THE CRAWLSPACE
A Collection Of Short Horror Stories

DARRYL DAWSON

AuthorHouse™
1663 Liberty Drive
Bloomington, IN 47403
www.authorhouse.com
Phone: 1-800-839-8640

© 2009 Darryl Dawson. All rights reserved.

No part of this book may be reproduced, stored in a retrieval system, or transmitted by any means without the written permission of the author.

First published by AuthorHouse 9/23/2009

ISBN: 978-1-4490-1084-3 (e)
ISBN: 978-1-4490-1083-6 (sc)

Printed in the United States of America
Bloomington, Indiana

This book is printed on acid-free paper.

To Mom, Dad & Marc

Acknowledgments

To my fifth-grade teacher, Mr. McBride, who first recognized my talents and gave them a gentle shove. To all my friends and co-workers at KPHO and KPNX, and everyone I have encountered along my long, arduous career in radio and television. To the Dawson/Rambo/Brown extended family throughout the U.S. To all the Mighty Gauchos of Narbonne High School, past, present and future. To Milli Thornton, for helping to get all of this started and for giving me a much harder shove. To all my fellow Afro-Punks…be you, and wave your Freak Flag high! To Rod Serling, Stephen King, Ray Bradbury, Langston Hughes, Clive Barker and the countless others who have shaped me. And to *you*, for buying this book and telling everyone how much you enjoyed it (you are doing that, aren't you?).

And finally, to one of my favorite teachers, Miss Wood.

Table of Contents

1. Hamburger Lady — 7
2. The Puppet Show — 15
3. The House With No Clocks — 35
4. I Am He Who Laughs Last — 47
5. The Crawlspace — 51
6. A Test Of Faith — 65
7. Trick — 73
8. I Scream, You Scream — 77
9. The Proper Technique — 93
10. Chien Sauvage — 103
11. Yellow — 113
12. Closing Time At Teddie's — 117
13. Connecting Flight — 129

Hamburger Lady

(From a note dated August 17, 1973, found in an envelope on the author's nightstand)

I want to tell you about the time I saw a ghost, and the things I've done at Newberry High School for which I am deeply ashamed.

If you think this an attempt to garner sympathy, that's not my intention, and besides, sympathy is not what I need right now. It won't do me any good. All I want to do is gain some kind of perspective on what I've seen and why I've seen it, for what's left of my peace of mind. Make what you will of it, but what I tell you is true, at least according to my understanding of truth.

My name is Orlando Wake. I'd been teaching literature at Newberry for twelve years.

Urban legends, I believe, are as much a part of high school culture as senior ditch day. I've heard plenty of accounts from students retelling the sordid stories of lost spirits in the gymnasium or the cafeteria or the girls' locker room, and as the stories get passed on from generation to generation they grow wilder and more grotesque in the decompression of translation.

Darryl Dawson

The stories I've heard flying about among the student body regarding the "Hamburger Lady" are as gruesome as an impressionable teenager can make them, but are actually rather mild in comparison to the facts, which after a few weeks of research I can now share with you.

Most of you are unfamiliar with Darius Maghee, and that wouldn't be surprising, because his life went mostly unnoticed. He worked in a slaughterhouse in Goodyear, Arizona in the mid-1920's, a son of a Scottish immigrant. Folks described him as a "quiet, pleasant gentleman" who, on the surface, didn't fit the profile of a murderer.

Very little is known about the prostitute he picked up one night in September 1928, but knowing what I know now, I could probably reach the conclusion that she was a beautiful, vibrant young woman who wanted the means, not the sex her activities provided. I think in spite of her position, she loved life very much. There's no doubt about that.

Maghee picked up that prostitute in Phoenix, strangled her, and brought her body to the slaughterhouse after hours where he processed it like the pigs and cows that met their fates behind its walls. This poor, desperate, unknown young woman was gutted, drained, and turned into ground meat. Her body was discovered the following day, and the slaughterhouse was shut down. It is unknown if any parts of her ended up in the meat supply.

That was according to Maghee's delirious, panicky confession to the authorities two months after he murdered the girl. He was hung in Florence Prison two years later, just twenty-nine years old. His last words were "God, I hope I never see her again," and it would be easy to interpret them as an expression of raw apathy for a young life, but I know that's not what he meant.

I know, because I know now what was haunting him, what made him confess. I've seen it in the halls of Newberry High School, which was built on the spot where the old slaughterhouse used to stand. For everyone who has passed through those halls, it was a shocking and amusing legend, but one that wouldn't manifest itself into reality for just anyone. Most of the student body believed the story was just some sick joke born in reaction to the Manson family murders from a couple of years back.

One who didn't was a young lady who I will only refer to as Daisy, a bright, warm, charismatic junior in my third period composition class.

There are certain women for whom men would forsake their morals, obligations, and even logic just to hold them close and kiss them, and Daisy fits that description. Maybe it's a little ironic that I refer to her as a woman, but she was all definitions of that to me. She was *beyond* desirable, womanly shaped beyond her peers, shameless in her conversation, coltish yet seething with quiet seduction. I was her teacher, yet I was no different from all the shy, pimple-faced boys in the room who wanted to sit as close to her as possible, with the exception that I was happily married, a father of a baby boy, and an authority figure in the community.

None of that mattered whenever I saw her, although I struggled with keeping my feelings in check for the sake of my profession if nothing else. I lost that struggle when I met her after school one day to discuss one of her papers and she professed her attraction to me with an openness and vulnerability I couldn't resist.

We had sexual relations for a month, and for that I am deeply sorry.

In all my years of teaching I've never sought out such relationships with students and even found the idea of doing so distasteful. So what made me want to satisfy my physical needs with a young woman twenty years younger on the desk of my own classroom? I wish I knew. Perhaps that ghost knows the answer.

It was Daisy who first told me the details of what the students knew about the ghost, the "Hamburger Lady" as they call her. It was after one of our late night "sessions" in Room 5 of the English building. With a twinkle in her eyes that revealed equal parts fascination and fear, she told me of the old meat packing plant and how a "female employee was stuffed into the meat grinder out of jealousy," in her words. I told her she was far too sophisticated to believe in such nonsense.

"My big brother saw it," she explained. "One day he got caught making out with some girl in the boy's bathroom, but he never got in trouble for it other than two hours of detention. The next night after football practice he saw it. He said it looked like a woman with bloody skin crawling on her hands and knees. Scared the crap out of him. It's been four years and he hasn't been the same since."

The Crawlspace

She went on to say that only men claim to have seen the Hamburger Lady, theorizing in her sweet way that it only wanted to terrorize the men because it was some kind of "women's lib" ghost, an otherworldly defender with the purpose of offsetting the social dominance of men. I found that to be both brilliant and funny. I'm not laughing now.

Two nights after that exchange I was in my classroom again waiting for Daisy with my wife at home believing I was "helping the basketball team at practice." I kept the lights off and the doors unlocked. I recall the clock reading 7:15, which meant that she was a few minutes late, and I had more time to sit in the dark and think about how wrong this was and the dreadful idea that it would be her father or my wife walking through that door. The darkness has a way of needling the conscience of a guilty man.

It was then that I heard something in the hallway that sounded like wet footsteps of bare feet--slow and deliberate, yet landing with an audible squish--moving from one end of the hallway to the other, passing right by my room. The squishing stopped on the other end of the hall and everything was silent again. My throat was drying up. I wanted to believe that there was no one on the entire campus but me and Daisy, but what was making that sound? I cracked open the door and peeked into the hallway. In the darkness, the glass panes above the building's main doors provided a dim aperture of light.

On the floor there was blood. Even in the semi-darkness I knew it couldn't be anything else. It was a long line of blood, thin and splotchy, like something one would expect from a body being dragged, stopped, then dragged again across the floor. The line started at my door, trailed up the hall, curved and ended at the east stairwell.

A sickness welled up inside me as I began to think of Daisy and why she was late.

I followed the thin trail of blood up the hallway, praying to God I wouldn't find what I thought would be on the other end. If anything had happened to that beautiful young lady I would never forgive myself.

At the base of the stairwell was something I did not expect. It wasn't Daisy or her father, nor was it my wife. It was no living thing at all.

It was coiled on the bottom steps of the stairwell on all fours, a nude, human form with mangled, furrowed skin glistening with an unforgiving red. Its torso appeared to be female, but its shapely form was tattered. Large chunks of flesh were ripped from its legs and back leaving exposed bone, and both of its feet were gone, ripped at the shins. If it had skin at all, it was stained with its blood. On its face (not much more than ragged, red strands) was a single eye, bloodshot and blue, that allowed its meager expression of agony and rage to reveal itself to me, accusing me of crimes of which only it knew. It crawled toward me, its fingerless hands squishing in its own bloody muck. Then it turned away from me and slithered up its own trail back down the hall, and disappeared into the darkness.

The Crawlspace

I only stood there, unable to speak, barely able to breathe. If such a creature came from God, then God should be punished.

I don't know how long I was standing there when I heard someone call my name, but I remember the sound that came from my throat—something between a scream and a swallow.

Daisy stood at the door of Room 5 apologizing for being late, staring with that irresistible lust in her eyes. I was in no mood to meet with her--my heart felt like it was turning inside out—but I needed company. Right then I needed someone warm and alive to hold in my arms and help remove the nightmare from my mind. I looked down at the floor and noticed the bloody stripe was no longer there. It's gone, I thought. Nothing there.

We went back into the classroom to make love. I didn't ask her about the Hamburger Lady, how it was described by people who've seen it. We didn't talk much at all. I just let her have her way with me as I did with her. We were on my desk and Daisy was on top of me when I closed my eyes, allowing my desire to take hold of me. I opened my eyes.

The Hamburger Lady was on top of me. Her cold, bludgeoned, bloody form. Her accusing eye.

I remember screaming, but I don't remember much else about that night. Daisy claims that I struck her across the face and tried to strangle her, but that couldn't be possible. I loved her, or at the very least, I liked her enough to never want to harm her. If I'm guilty of

Darryl Dawson

anything, it's having an inappropriate relationship with a teenage girl.

Anyway that's a moot point. My wife is gone and I'll never see my baby boy again. I'll never teach again. By no means am I whining about it; I brought all this upon myself and I deserve all the shame. But those misfortunes are mild in comparison to what I'm dealing with now. The house I tried to make with my family is empty and lonely beyond anything I could imagine. And yet I'm never alone.

In my dreams and in my waking hours I see her, crawling, oozing, staring at me with vengeance burning from her eye. She never speaks, but her gaze, her awful, blood-drenched presence, tells me all I need to know about my shameful life. I thought when I left Newberry High I had left her there, a salacious fairy tale to be told and retold to curious young minds. But she's real…Oh God, she's *real!* Even now as I write this, I can hear the *squish-squish-squish* back and forth and up and down the walls and the floors. I hear it again. She watches me like a prison guard, her eye… *her eye.* I can't go into my own bedroom anymore. She won't let me sleep.

She's here.

She won't leave me alone. And now I know what she wants from me.

For the last time, I'm sorry. You'll find my body in the basement.

The Puppet Show

The last time anyone would see Tyrone and Delta was shortly before the long drive back to Arizona. Theirs was one of dozens of unremarkable cars rolling across the desert highway, heading towards the piercing light of pre-sunset in the direction of California or away from it towards the sleepy, old West charm of Arizona.

Delta's eyes blinked open behind her convenience store sunglasses. "Tucson?" she yawned. The stunning, copper-skinned black woman of post-college youth, vacationing from her nursing job, stretched in the passenger seat as best she could, shaking the short, stretchy curls of her brown hair and fighting a nagging stiffness in her neck. She pulled off her cheap shades revealing eyes the color of freshly-brewed cups of tea.

"About a hundred twenty miles left," said Ty, who unlike his girlfriend had a year of college left. "We're gonna stop here."

She sighed and nodded. Gas and rest stops were frequent in Ty's crusty, noisy old Audi sedan, but much to her amazement it got them to California and back.

Delta squinted at the dreary landscape rolling by...the sand-colored prickly pears...the angular Joshua trees...the spiny corpses of dried-up bushes waiting for a gust of wind to carry them along.

The highway sign appeared with its simple message in white reflective paint: Whispering Drum Road, 1 ½ Miles, Exit 214. A blue and white "gas" symbol hung beneath it. Behind it was another sign, not from the state, adorned with a smiling clown's face:

Visit The House of Smiles Puppet Show! Next Exit! Don't Miss It!

"Gas and a puppet show! Ain't America great?" quipped Ty, pushing his prescription shades up higher on his nose. He was a clever, sensitive young white hipster who preferred the stubble on his face, believing it made him look tougher than he actually was.

"I need a piss break more than a puppet show," she retorted, then mused over the sign they just passed. Whispering Drum. A name so beautiful to Delta she couldn't possibly forget it. She wondered where she'd heard or seen it before.

They pulled into the only gas station within two hundred feet of the Whispering Drum exit. There were only two pumps, trimmed in red and utilizing the old spinning black dials with white numbers, looking like they could still pump leaded gas. Each had a small cardboard sign attached with duct tape just above the Texaco logo, with the message "PAY FIRST INSIDE" handwritten in thick, black ink. The garage behind them was coated with dust, empty for years.

The Crawlspace

To the left and across the street was an auto salvage yard teeming with gutted cars. A tall, bulky man was closing and locking the sliding chain-link gate. He was over six feet tall and built round but athletic like a shot-putter, and he wore a gray shop uniform spotted with dark stains and an Australian aborigine tattoo covering the back of his shaven head like a pointy, black vine. He stared back at Delta as he walked. His thin lips were pursed in a dour, stoic expression and his eyes were sharp and wolfen. She watched him stride diligently toward, then disappear behind, the back of the building to the right of the garage, which was decorated with wall-sized renderings of grinning circus clowns.

"This place looks empty," she said. "Maybe we ought to try the next one."

"The next one isn't for another seventy-five miles," Ty assured her. He didn't catch a glimpse of the big, bald, tattooed man. "I don't want to chance it. I guess we're supposed to pay in there."

"Ty, there's nobody here..." She hoped the urgency in her voice would change his mind.

"Hey, what's wrong?" He put his hand on her shoulder and waited for an answer, but none came. "Didn't you say you needed a piss break?"

She had forgotten about that. It wasn't an urgent need, but necessary. "Okay, but let's make it quick. This place just...feels funny."

"Sitting in a puddle of your own piss in the front seat would feel a lot funnier!"

Delta smiled as they walked toward the brick-red and canary-yellow building, reassured by his corny remark, but not for very long.

There were more of the garish clown faces greeting them on the inside of the shop, appearing on t-shirts, shot glasses, kitchen magnets and the various knick-knacks they would find in typical roadside gift shops along their journey. There were also a wide variety of marionettes, two-feet high and smaller, wooden and plastic, made in parts of the world where labor was a penny on the dollar. They hung like broken scarecrows from their strings, waiting with bright expressions to be picked up and manipulated.

"Welcome to the House of Smiles!" chimed a soft, elderly voice that reminded Delta of Winnie the Pooh. It came from a thin, wrinkled man sitting behind a counter near the entrance. He wore a checkerboard bow tie and bright blue suspenders. His face bore an empty smile with yellowing teeth and distant, dark, cadaverous eyes.

Ty wanted to look away from the odd caretaker but found no one else in the shop he could address. "Those gas pumps out there," he asked, "do they work?"

The old man tilted his head, not offended but amused by the young visitor's silly question. "Why, of course they do!"

Ty handed the man his debit card. "Fill-up, please?"

The Crawlspace

"Oh, I'm sorry. Cash only," said the elderly man, his voice dripping with a mortician's sympathy.

Delta was relieved for a moment, until her boyfriend reached into his pocket and pulled out a pair of twenty dollar bills.

"Fill-up it is!" The old man took his money and with one index finger punched the keys of a cash register that looked about as old as the pumps. "Admission is free with a fill-up."

"I just need to use your restroom," Delta interjected, wanting to spend as little time as possible in this odd little shop full of hanging puppets.

The smiling old man reached underneath the counter and produced a wooden plank with a single key attached. "Outside," he lilted, "behind the garage!"

Just a second of eye contact with the old man made Delta feel unnaturally cold. As she took the clumsy key fob and hastened to the door she overheard Ty. "So where's the show?" he asked.

Don't! she thought, but she didn't say it. She walked out into the heat and the dust, and as the front door banged behind her she thought she heard the old man's labored, childlike voice replying, "Downstairs."

Delta stepped out of the restroom (cleaner and tidier than what she expected) and glanced out at the junkyard across the street. Rusted, wrecked bodies of sedans and trucks at least a decade old, and some newer. One SUV that looked a little too new.

The Audi was still waiting by the gas pumps, and Ty was not filling it up. She sighed. Spending more time than necessary in this weird place in the middle of nowhere was not in her plans.

She shoved open the door and scanned the clothing racks and shelves of Native American crafts and puppets of all types and sizes. She couldn't see him.

"Was that your boyfriend?"

Startled, she turned and saw the old man still sitting behind the counter, his pallid face still baring that tarnished, empty grin and those empty eyes. In front of him was a small television monitor and a metal box with a long-necked microphone. She recalled that feeling in her throat when she was four years old and swallowed a marble. "Um…yeah, he was…just here," she stammered. "Did you see him filling up the car?"

"Oh, no. He's downstairs enjoying the show! He said he'd fill it up when he got back!"

Shit, she thought. "How long does the show last?"

It was just a slight tilt of his head, yet for some reason it made Delta's heart sink. "Not long," he almost sung, looking like a cartoon drawn by a psychopath. "Not long at all!"

Exasperation and a feeling that could only be described as "the willies" were circulating through Delta. She'd drive off and leave him if…no, she wouldn't. Too many good times between them and too much future ahead of them. Too much love. And the keys were in his pocket.

The Crawlspace

"Listen, is it okay if I go down there and look for him? We really have to go."

The old man's smile widened, and it looked painful. "Of course you can! Your fill-up admission is good for two! Right back there!"

He pointed to a white door with a picture of a clown's head in the back of the room. The clown was bald with a tiny, pointed hat on its head and manic green eyes and its tongue sticking out of its red-lipped mouth in mischievous defiance. Beneath its tongue were the words, *"HOUSE OF SMILES! ENTER."* And below it, a smaller sign:

"Do NOT touch the puppets!"

As Delta approached the entrance she tried to come to grips with the silence of the place, the nightmarish decorum, the weirdness of the whole situation, and hoping that it would end like most of her dreams ended—inconclusive, puzzling. She didn't want it to be real, because it certainly didn't feel that way.

"Wake Uh-up!" the old man's voice chimed behind her.

She thought he was talking to her, but he was speaking into the microphone. The glow of the monitor gave a faint illumination to his waxy face. He gave her a wink.

She touched the doorknob and a loud buzzing rumbled from behind it, making her jerk her hand away and look down at her feet to see if the floor was wet. She looked back at the old man, who was deactivating the magnetic lock from an unseen button and silently nodding at her as if to say, *"Go on, child. It's fun. Go on."* She pulled the door open and the buzzing stopped.

An uncovered, low-watt bulb burned and barely illuminated the stairwell from overhead, bringing an ugly orange glow to the faded antique wallpaper. As Delta swallowed and descended down the spiral flight of metal steps the door closed behind her and locked. The wooden soles of her flip-flops made a dull clang on every step, thirteen or fourteen times. She came to the grey door at the base of the stairs and it too was monitored by a magnetic lock, and it was buzzing. She pushed it open and called Ty's name. The faint sound of cheerful calliope music wafted from behind.

Like it did for everyone before her, the door closed behind her and locked.

And upstairs, the old man had turned his monitor to channel 4, and the middle-aged woman was there just like Army had promised. And today would be a wonderful day. Three more...*three!* He was confident in the man who called himself Army, the big, strong bull who supplied his special entertainment. He was already downstairs looking for the other two.

For now, he stared at a short-haired forty-year-old woman lying on a floor next to a white chair. He adjusted the radio frequency to make sure she could hear him. "Wake uh-up!" he whispered again into the microphone, pulling a string in her brain. He licked his lips. It was time to give her something to do.

"Brush," he said with a cool, calm hiss. "Brush your hair..."

The Crawlspace

Delta knew what a funhouse was, and she had many reasons to not like them. In her childhood visits to the state fair she preferred the stomach-stirring speed and screaming energy of roller coasters and thrill rides to the spooky, bump-in-the-night surprises of those poorly-named attractions. She expected one when she opened the door...a dark, claustrophobic place filled with distortioning mirrors and disorienting lights.

Instead she was in a corridor with ten doors on either side, like a hotel floor. The carpet was thin and patterned with paisley-like splashes of pea-soup green, white and black, and the walls were covered with the same fading wallpaper as the stairwell--a dull assembly of brown, tan and olive stripes. The light came from diamond-shaped ceiling lights overhead. The air smelled heavy and dank, almost rotten. And the music—a jaunty, pipe organ soundtrack to someone's invisible circus—seemed to hang in that stagnant air from a distant place.

The image of the old guy at the counter crept into her mind. Who was he telling to wake up?

"Ty...Ty, let's go...Ty?"

Whispering Drum...Whispering Drum...

The hospital...where she worked...

A young man...found by the police...bleeding, laughing...walking along the highway...all cut up...

"Ty...don't play games with me, please? We really have to go...Ty, where the hell are you?"

Whispering Drum...

Young man...bleeding, laughing...brought back into town...killed himself...smiling face...

Now she was remembering. Delta felt a tiny explosion of terror in her gut.

They weren't sure if the man who was found walking along the highway east of Whispering Drum Road, bleeding and delirious, had been stabbed or had tried to escape a razor wire fence. He never spoke to anyone, but all he did was laugh. They didn't find out until after he hung himself that he had been reported missing for several months.

She tried the door directly across from the one that closed behind her. The scuffed, bronze doorknob felt like it was barely attached as she twisted it, and stepped in.

The lights along the wall came on by themselves when she entered the room, and they bathed the room in a yellowish-brown glow. She left the door open in case Ty would come walking in, equally freaked out and ready to bolt. She hoped it would be him around the corner of the short entry way, ready to spring like a horror movie cat and say "boo!" and scare the crap out of her. It would make her mad, but at least it would make sense.

Delta peered around the corner and saw the display.

It was a small stage, separated from the rest of the room by a wall of clear plastic from the ceiling to its base. A single spotlight was shining on a white, plastic lawn chair.

Next to the chair, lying face-first on the floor, was a short-haired woman.

The woman moved, tried to get up. She was a slender woman in her forties with short-cropped blonde hair wearing a tank top and shorts. Her face was attractive, yet gaunt and sagging with despair. She stood up and turned her head. There was a small incision on the back of her neck just below the base of her skull, not stitched up, but not bloody.

Delta pounded against the wall of Plexiglas that curtained off the stage. "Are you okay?" she yelled, but the woman inside ignored her as the despair on her face was turning to wide, red-eyed terror as she slumped onto the chair.

"What's going on?" Delta pleaded. *"What is this place?"* She thought she heard something that sounded like a gunshot out in the hallway.

The woman on the stage opened her mouth without uttering a sound. Her fright-colored face darted around in all directions until it settled on a shopping bag, plain and square, standing just out of the spotlight. She trembled.

And then she began to smile. Her eyes remained wide and red and she shook her head back and forth as her quivering fingers reached into the bag. But she smiled; it was a forced, unnatural smile, wide and gruesome.

She pulled out something that looked like a hair brush, but instead of bristles it had nails, long and thick and sharp and infected with specks of rust.

The woman laughed. Through the clear, plastic wall Delta could hear her high-pitched, manic giggle. It sounded inhuman, like it was coming from a place miles away from joy or amusement. The laughter of the mad.

No horror movie she had ever endured could prepare Delta for what she was about to see.

She saw the woman plunge the nail brush into her scalp and carve bleeding furrows from her forehead down to the back of her neck, again and again, shaking and laughing, glistening red stripes dripping down her face, specks dotting her shoulders. Bleeding. Laughing...

It wasn't until she was back in the hallway with the ugly carpet and the brown wall and the beveled door at her back that she was even aware she had run, felt the shortness of her breath and the crawly feeling in her face. It didn't seem like too far of a distance. It wasn't far enough.

She opened the next door and ran in. The room was empty and its Plexiglas chamber unoccupied. She tried the room directly across from it. Also empty. Another room was not empty but it should have been, with a decaying, smiling corpse of someone who apparently used a power drill on his own neck. It was in this room where she heard another noise from outside--a door slamming shut.

The Crawlspace

Something else was there, she knew, she felt. And it would find her. Maybe already found Ty. And it was hiding.

Back in the foreboding hallway, she found the plain, grey door through which she entered and twisted the silver door handle with manic urgency, unable to move it more than an inch up or down. She pounded her fists against it and screamed until she sobbed and gave up. She looked at the long, ugly hallway, ten doors to a side, and understood.

Behind one of those doors was the man…the beast…that was following her. And behind another door, perhaps…God willing…was an escape. With or without her boyfriend, she had to find it. *"Swim or drown, you gotta jump in the water,"* as her mother used to say.

She gathered herself. Fifteen doors to go. Swim or drown.

The old man was watching his favorite television show, the one he watched every day from the monitor on the counter, his wrinkled cheeks glowing red with delight. The image on channel 16 was of a young man, still wearing his glasses, slumped against a plastic patio chair in a dim, empty room. Army had found him, prepared him, and now he was asleep, waiting for his wake-up call.

He wondered how this one would go. Not by the Nail-Brush this time—Army always saved that for the women. Perhaps this one would chew through the electrical cord. Army hated watching that but the old man loved it, the way the lights would dim and sparks popped and sizzled in the air like a fireworks show. So what would it be? The power drill? The screwdriver? The acid? Army always had a surprise.

The man in the glasses was ready. Now all that was needed was Grandpa's soothing voice to call him to act, but he waited this time. He knew the girl was looking for her friend, and he relished in the idea that she would find him and witness his performance before Army would find her too. What a lovely consequence.

The day was getting dark and there would be no more customers, no distractions. He waited by the TV and fantasized about how it would all happen, staring into the screen with palpable, happy intensity.

His heart skipped a beat when he saw a shadow creeping into the room, edging up toward the man in the chair. It was the girl. Sucking the blood from his cracked lip, he pulled the microphone down toward his mouth.

"Wake Uh-up!"

Hope is cruel. It has a way of reaching out its hand to rescue you from whatever dire situation you find yourself in, then pulling its hand back and giving you the finger, then reaching out again, then pulling back, and repeating those gestures over and over to test your will.

When Delta walked in the room and saw Tyrone, for a moment she had hope, and then she didn't. He

The Crawlspace

was sitting, drained and immobile, on a white patio chair next to a metal watering can behind a clear, solid wall, and for a moment she believed he was dead. He didn't respond to her frantic pounding and raw-throated screams. His eyes were shut. His glasses sat slightly crooked on his slack face.

His fingers began to twitch, his eyes blinked open into disbelieving squints, and he stirred. Delta felt Hope standing over her again, reaching out its unpredictable hand.

"How do we get out of here?" she sobbed. "Ty...can you hear me?"

Ty tried pushing himself out of the chair and it seemed to require every ounce of strength he had left. He crumpled to the floor, unable or unwilling to stand. The words he spoke were muffled by the plastic wall between him and his girlfriend, but she could read his lips and the terrified expression on his face. "No..." he whispered to no one, "No..."

She watched him shiver, balled up in a fetal position, his hands over his ears, his mouth stretched open as if trying to scream. Or perhaps he was screaming.

Delta's confusion sparked and caught fire, and she was determined to tear down that curtain of acrylic if it meant shattering every bone in her body. She rammed it with her shoulder, kicked it, pushed and pulled it, screamed at it, cried on it. It didn't move or crack. The room, like all the other rooms, was absent of furniture or any items that could be useful in breaking it down. Her flesh and her fear were not enough. She fell to her knees and kicked off her broken flip-flops as a tingling pain simmered in her shoulder and elbow. She glanced at Ty, wondering what she could say to help him, to soothe his pain.

Ty looked back at her, and on his face was a sick, unwholesome smile.

He stood up and started laughing behind clenched teeth, his eyes darting from side to side, as if his laughter was hurting him and he couldn't make it stop. As he took a seat again in the patio chair he began to quiver and the pitch of his manic laughter grew higher. He fought every urge to pick up the metal watering can beside him, but he couldn't help himself. The liquid inside the can sloshed around to the rhythm of his shaking as he leaned back and held it above his chest. He took one last look at Delta. The look on his face told her that sanity was a road he would never travel again.

He tilted the can and poured. The stream of acid splashed and melted into his body, sending small plumes of acrid smoke into the sealed chamber. His laughter turned into a muffled scream until it stopped abruptly. The can dropped to the floor, its contents burning the wood panels to a black finish. The chair sank beneath him and blended with the bubbling muck that was once his innards.

And the smile never left his face.

In the semi-darkness of the room, all the joy, all the sweet memories of the trip, all the little warm emotions and the big, delicious desires...all of it was drained from her and swept into the shadows, unreachable, gone, and leaving her soul stinging with an abrupt, icy cold.

The Crawlspace

Delta stumbled through the foyer and back into the fierce lights of the hallway, falling to the carpet, catching the soft stench of old dust with each stuttering breath, shaking and trying to forget. Trying to understand.

Who are the puppets? And who tilts the cross that holds the strings? Where is the hand that pries open the mouth...?

She felt a presence behind her. Her eyes darted to each laughing clown face sewn into the pattern of the carpet. She felt the memory of that marble in her throat again as she turned and looked up.

The man she didn't know was named Army, the large man with the wolf-like eyes and the tattoo on his shaved head, stood over her with what appeared to be a shotgun. The look on his face was warm, apologetic.

"I promise you, this won't hurt," he said.

She rolled away, the first shot missing her by inches as she stood up and ran toward the end of the hall, no longer needing to know what was the purpose of the place she was in. The second shot caught her in the thigh, tripping her. She grabbed her leg expecting to find a hole and a bullet, but instead felt a short tube that in her moment of pure fear she thought was bone at first. She pulled the tube...the syringe...out of her leg.

She got up and ran again until she reached the last door at the end of the hallway on the left. She wasn't sure why she chose that one but instinct was all she had left, for if there was to be an escape, and life, for her, it must be found in this room. And quickly, because she was starting to feel light-headed and tasted a strange medicine flavor in her mouth.

But this room was brighter than the others with the plastic chambers, although the brightness was dimming. She saw what looked like an operating table, or perhaps it was just a mattress, stained with little drops of red, on a cheap dining table. Next to the table (her head felt heavy) was a tray of surgical instruments and a small cardboard box (eyes cloudy) filled with little plastic fingertip-sized pieces.

A voice behind her saying, "This won't hurt, and it won't take long," was the last thing Delta heard before she passed out.

There were no dreams, no make-believe place for her conscious mind to take refuge. There was no sense of time. It felt like only a few seconds before she was able to open her eyes, and when she did, the solitary light bulb that hung over her blasted its soft, fiery glare, stealing space from the fuzzy darkness. She thought--wanted to believe--she could make out God's face in the stinging radiance. She listened for angels. If there were any to be found, they were as silent as the dead bodies they came from.

Her head ached in two places; between her eyes there was a dull soreness and in the back of her head was a pain that was a little different...a kind of itching, as though some creature had burrowed into the back of her neck and made a home between her brain and the base of her skull. It didn't hurt, but it didn't feel good.

The Crawlspace

She sat upright, closing her eyes, trying to find moisture in her mouth. She wanted to be home in bed, with Ty lying next to her so she could wake him up and tell him about the weird, scary dream she had about him killing himself with acid and how he smiled as he was dying. She opened her eyes and saw the light above her reflecting off the clear plastic wall.

"BRUSSSSHH!"

The voice seemed to vibrate from inside of her head. Her whole body shook.

"BRUSSSHH!"

She didn't want to stand up, but she did. She wanted to scream, but she couldn't. She didn't want to sit down in the white plastic chair next to her in the little room, but she did. She began thinking about the short, stretchy curls of her hair, and she didn't know why.

The voice in her head was gentle, elderly. It pounded from behind her ears.

"BRUSH YOUR HAIR, MY SWEET! IT'S TIME TO BRUSH YOUR HAIR!"

She convulsed, fighting the urges. She didn't know what was in the brown paper bag to her left, but her trembling fingers nearly shredded the bag to get at what was inside. She held the thing tightly in her hand, and the feeling came over her.

A hair brush, with long, sharp, steel nails where the fibers should have been.

"BRUSH YOUR HAIR, MY SWEET!"

Darryl Dawson

She was thinking about her hair, how pretty it would look, how the blood would make it beautiful. And a wide gruesome smile came to her face.

The House With No Clocks

Leo brushed the snot from the brim of his lip. He had just gotten up from his nap in the park, where he dreamed that he was living in a dark, lonely house with mismatched furniture. It was Christmas time in his dream, and underneath an artificial tree caked with fake snow was his gift, a set of luggage. Something in the street woke him up before he could touch his gift. He believed the dream meant that he was going somewhere, that his life would change. He always believed that.

The grimy homeless man, who not long ago was fit, handsome and financially getting by, only had another mile or so of walking to go before he would reach the soup kitchen on Washington Street, but he wasn't sure he could make it this time. The unfiltered sun compounded his misery, making a spring day feel like the dead of summer. His neck felt like it had been rubbed raw with sandpaper. His sack of everything he had left was heavy on his shoulder.

Many people have told Leo Franklin that the best way to get through this low point in his life was through prayer, but Leo never prayed much, and when he did it was always out of a dutiful "when-in-Rome" respect. Leo believed in God, but he also believed in Gambling and that old, misinterpreted axiom, "Money isn't everything." Every dollar he had earned and saved in his thirty-seven years was now circulating in Vegas, Laughlin and a couple of Indian reservations. He never conquered his compulsion. Leo lived too much in fear of missing "the big one" to realize that money is everything, and now he was almost nothing.

He was only able to make it as far as a bus stop on 7th Avenue when he cried out in pain--his legs were cramping up from lack of hydration. He sat on the shaded bench and gave his calf muscles a massage which did little good. He couldn't walk, but he had to; he would miss a meal otherwise. For now he would have to rest and order his empty stomach not to think about dinner for awhile. Besides, he wanted to dream again.

A bright red pickup truck pulled out of traffic into the bus lane where Leo was sitting. The driver, a thin, college-aged man with spiky, red hair almost as bright as the truck, quickly got out and opened up a cooler secured to the truck bed by bungee cord, reached in and pulled out a bottle of water from the melting collection of ice. "Here you go, man," he said, offering the bottle to Leo.

Leo felt a twinge of pain as he twisted the bottle cap in his calloused fingers. He drank vigorously, without stopping to enjoy the refreshment. He was too tired, too famished, and too desperate to enjoy it, or to say thanks.

The Crawlspace

"You want another one?" asked the red-haired man when he was finished. He looked like a leprechaun that ditched his regular wardrobe for a dress shirt and tie. His nose was turned upward and his pupils were the color of Heineken bottles.

"Yeah, sure," Leo mumbled, and the odd-looking young man reached back into the cooler for another bottle.

"You looked like you were having a hard time out here. Do you need a ride?"

"Can you get me to Blessed Heart?"

"Sure! No problem at all! C'mon, I'll help you!"

He handed Leo the second bottle, draped his arm over his shoulders and limped him to the passenger side of the truck, which was still running in the bus lane. Leo pulled himself in and basked in the cool, pine-smelling air. With his clothes speckled with various unknown stains and smelling like a wet piece of steel, he almost felt apologetic for sitting in the immaculate cabin. It had been a while since he saw the inside of a vehicle as clean as this.

The red-haired man settled behind the wheel and started out into traffic. "My name's Elric. What's yours?"

"I'm Leo. Thanks for the water." He closed his eyes.

"Don't mention it. I help folks like you every day. How long you been down on your luck?"

Leo had to think about that one. When was the last time he saw his wife and kids? When did the tow trucks and the moving vans come to his house? When did the urge to play blackjack become more important than eating? "About a year-and-a-half, I think," he answered.

Elric shook his head. "What a shame. It happens so fast, doesn't it? Everything's running like clockwork, you're living the American Dream, and then poof! All gone. What was it? Drugs...drinking?"

"Nah, nothing like that. I just lost some money, that's all."

"Oh, a gambler, then."

Leo turned to stare at the neatly-dressed man at the wheel. He wasn't big enough to be a bookie's goon, and too young to work for the I.R.S. "Who wants to know?" he asked.

"I'm just making conversation!" There was a cunning innocence in Elric's grin. "Nothing to be ashamed of, really. You're just a guy who takes high risks in search of a high reward. Those are the most successful people in life. You'll find your breaks, no doubt you will!"

Leo noticed they had driven well beyond his intended destination and were headed to the freeway. "Hey, I think you missed…"

"Don't worry about that. I have a homeless shelter of my own."

Leo gave him a puzzled look. "Mister, I really have to eat right now!"

"You'll get plenty to eat, I promise."

The Crawlspace

An odd feeling crept over Leo, one that cast a shadow over his trust of the man driving the truck. "Look, you can drop me off here…"

"Nonsense! My shelter has so much more to offer than that lousy place. Let me ask you something. If I were to give you one hundred dollars, how would you spend it?"

He said nothing, contemplating that last statement with disbelief. A stranger in a sparkling new truck was about to give him money without being begged, and not just a quarter or a worn-out dollar bill, but a hundred bucks? It didn't seem possible.

"Think about it," said Elric. "One hundred dollars. That's probably more money than you've had in a while, isn't it?"

"You're shittin' me."

Elric laughed with a kind of boisterousness that seemed almost staged. "I assure you, I am not 'shitting' you, Leo. Here's the deal. I'm going to give you a hundred dollars to take a look at my place. No catch, no fine print…just walk through the front door and the money's all yours. Does that sound good to you?"

It did sound good to Leo. He had only utilized a couple of homeless shelters and was offered nothing more than food, used clothes, job placement counseling and prayer. Here was something he could really use! His mind raced. If he cleaned himself up enough to be let into Fort McDowell, all he needed was a few minutes at the blackjack tables and he'd be on his feet again. No, even better than that…what about a hundred Powerball tickets?

Still, Leo was a smart man. "What's inside this place you got?"

Elric took a breath in search of the right word. "Fulfillment. A chance to live out your heart's desire, for a nominal price."

Leo wasn't sure what that meant, and didn't really care. Maybe he'd do the scratchers instead of the Powerball tickets; they pay out more. "Well," he pondered, "for a hundred bucks, it sounds pretty easy."

Elric glanced at him with an affable, worldly-wise smile. "Easy, indeed! I'd say it's the easiest decision you'll ever make!"

They drove for another twenty minutes then exited onto a lonely, uneven street surrounded by farmland and small horse ranches, arriving a couple of miles later to a circular, solitary, single-level grey structure (it could have been black if not for years of weathering). The enormous wooden building was surrounded by a barren yard for twenty yards around it, as if the grass knew where not to grow. It had no mailbox, no numbers for an address…from all appearances, the oversized, windowless hut was unadorned by anything except a dozen or so crows serving as living gargoyles on the roof.

Leo's eyes widened as they approached. To him, it resembled one of those haunted houses he used to read about in comic books as a kid. At first the deal seemed pretty reasonable: walk through the front door, get a hundred bucks. Now he wasn't so sure.

The Crawlspace

"I know," said Elric as the truck pulled to a stop in the driveway. "It looks a little run down, doesn't it? Well, I can assure you, there's no reason to feel intimidated. Once you're inside, you won't even remember the outside." He reached a hand into the pocket of his neatly-pressed pants. "And I gave you my word I would make it worth your while didn't I?"

He pulled out a sizeable wad of bills from which he took a fresh C-note from the top. Smiling, he handed it to Leo, who accepted it with trembling hands amid thoughts of making a run for it. He turned the money over in his hands and held it up to the light to check the watermark. It was real. He changed his mind about running, mainly because he was miles from town anyway, but also because if he did, the funny-looking guy would probably want his money back. He'd had enough of creditors, legitimate and questionable, chasing him around for money. Besides, what could possibly be in that house that was so dangerous?

"The front door is right there," said Elric. "You go on ahead. I'll be right behind you."

Leo stuffed the money in his pocket. "Okay. Thanks."

"No, thank you!" Elric replied with a warm, mischievous smile.

Leo got out and walked up to the door of the old, weather-beaten place. One of the crows turned to look at him and cawed. It's alright, he thought, it's just a house.

He was close enough to hear the sounds from inside, and he stopped. His jaw went slack and his heart briefly forgot to beat. The noises, familiar noises, put him in a state of disbelief. He turned to look for the red-haired man, but he and his truck were gone. The hairs on his arm bristled as he stood at the door listening...

...listening to the faint electronic tones that beckoned him, the unmistakable harmonies of slot machines...

Slot machines! He twisted the egg-shaped doorknob and walked inside.

Standing in the room, he felt the sounds surrounding him, filling him with lust and adrenaline. The swirling, four-chord symphonies brought him back to that place in his mind when it wasn't so bad, when it was only the grocery money, before his life was ruined. His eyes glazed over in amazement. He started to chuckle. The door behind him closed by itself, locked, then disappeared, but Leo was too enraptured to notice.

The casino was beautiful and noisy, stacked with row after row of slot machines of every denomination and brand. It was bustling, but not crowded. There were plenty of empty seats for whatever action he desired, and the persistent clanking of coins in metal trays meant that the machines were paying out with regularity.

Leo kept waiting for the security guards to come and hustle him out of the place, but none would come. He noticed some of the clientele were dressed similarly to him, or worse in some cases. He felt like he belonged.

He reached into his pocket and pulled out the precious 100-dollar bill. It was time to get lucky.

The Crawlspace

Strolling with childlike excitement he went in search of the cheapest blackjack tables in the house, and had difficulty finding them. He could feel those two bottles of water building up inside him and looked around for a restroom but saw no signs. He turned and looked behind him.

The smile drained from his face as his excitement twisted into confusion. The room looked as though it had expanded by about five hundred square feet. There were more machines and more patrons in the sudden space. He couldn't have been walking that long.

He pressed the knuckles of his thumbs against his eyelids and blamed the heat. Regaining his mental balance, he continued wandering looking for a waitress or some kind of attendant.

He found a sad-looking elderly woman tapping the buttons on a Deuces Wild video poker machine, staring into the monitor as though it were a dead relative in a casket. "Excuse me," he said, "do you know where the restrooms are?"

The woman never looked up from her game. "I don't know," she replied, unbothered but spiritless.

Leo was growing frustrated and was unmoved by the old woman's demeanor. "Jesus," he muttered, "you'd think they could at least…"

Before he could finish, the sad woman hit a royal flush of diamonds. The machine roared its congratulations with a loud school-bell alarm. The number on the credit meter swelled to incredible proportions. "Wow! You hit it!" Leo shouted, laying his hand on her shoulder. "Congratulations, lady! How much is that worth?"

The lines on the woman's face seemed to grow deeper, and her left eye blinked out a single, lonely tear. She seemed exhausted, looking back at him with eyes so red they looked painful. "I have to keep playing," she sobbed. "None of this is worth anything. I have to keep playing."

Leo shuddered and backed away from the woman, who patiently waited for the alarm to stop so she could continue. Leo looked around again. The room was now even larger, feeling like an electric forest. The walls were gone.

Leo ran, dizzy and helpless through the endless rows of slots. The blackjack tables, wherever they were, would have to wait. For now, his only desire was to find a way out. He pleaded for help from the weary gamblers around him, who either ignored him or looked back at him with an all-consuming sorrow. Some of them didn't move at all. Leo didn't want to think that they might be dead, or that any of this was real, or that he was trapped.

He stopped somewhere in the midst of this infinite landscape to gather his breath and his thoughts. The beeps, dings and dongs that sounded so pleasant before were now the discordant soundtrack of his living nightmare. He put his hands to his ears to shut it all out when he felt a hand on his shoulder and spun around.

"Leo!"

It was Elric, smiling broadly and dressed in a black suit. "So glad I caught up with you. I hope you can forgive me for being such an ungracious host!" The

The Crawlspace

spiky, red hair didn't look like hair anymore; his head was crowned with steel barbs covered in blood. "Have any luck so far?"

Leo stared at him in horror. "Where am I?"

Elric reacted with his strange laughter again. "You know, I get asked that a lot, and I always give the same answer. Where you are is exactly where you belong."

"I want to get out of here. Where's the door?"

"Sorry," he replied, shaking his head in mock regret. "I pay you to go in. Getting out's a whole different song and dance, big man!"

Leo reached in his pocket and pulled out the hundred-dollar bill. "Look, I'll give you your money back, just let me out of here! Please!"

"Don't be ridiculous! That's yours! It's always been yours. Besides, it'll come back to me eventually." He laughed again.

Leo stared out into the vastness. It was far larger than the place he thought he was walking into. It looked like a mirror reflecting a mirror—it had no end. Dread consumed and digested him.

Elric pointed to an unoccupied Red, White & Blue machine. "Go ahead, have a seat. It's much more fun if you participate."

Leo was now starting to understand that the precious commodity he called "choice" was left outside with the sunlight. He sat at the machine and loaded the bill into the feeder.

The credits on the meter counted upward…a hundred, four hundred, two thousand…greater than the denomination. At 2500, he felt queasy. 5000, a sadness that expanded in his heart like a spill. 6000, physical and emotional numbness. 7000, no more will to live. When it finally stopped at 8742, his soul was drained.

He turned his sad, reddened eyes to Elrich, but he was already walking away.

He pushed the "Max Credits" button, and the wheels spun. Red 7, White 7, Blue 7. He hit the jackpot on his first spin.

But it didn't matter. He had to keep playing.

I Am He Who Laughs Last

"Okay, Rick, Diane, we'll toss it back to you, but before we do I'm going to attempt something called an ollie. Pretty simple trick, anybody can do it! I've been practicing a little bit here...Okay, ready? Here we go!"

Lance Harlan paused the video on his iPod at that point and laughed, knowing what was going to happen next. He couldn't help it. The final twenty seconds of the fifth most popular clip in the brief history of viral videos always played out in his mind as vividly as ever, and the tight, high-pitched laughter squeezed out of him in spasms. Rookie news reporter on skateboard. Wile E. Coyote reborn. Thud. He laughed until he wheezed and stroked his long, brown, spongy beard. It never gets old.

His laughter kept him warm in the quiet, frosty coolness of a late autumn night at the edge of Ray Russell Park, a drab, lonely playground in the daylight hours that served as a pharmaceutical supermarket after midnight. Lance, whose twenty-eighth birthday present was a job delivering pizzas, was neither a buyer nor a seller, but he somehow had a place here. It was a nice, temporary resting spot for him to think about things, like his dad's guitar, the fiancée who called off their wedding plans, and other parts of his life that have been destroyed. That video shed tiny pin lights of joy on those thoughts, but mainly it perplexed him. Who is that guy? Who was he? Does anybody know?

He watched it again..."*Okay, ready? Here we go!*" Pause.

This time he recalled the crazy sounds the reporter made after landing belly first on the wooden skate ramp, almost like a barking seal. He laughed again. Must have been painful. Hilarious. His calloused fingers stroked the tiny grooves of the guitar string in his pocket and his mood changed. He missed that old guitar, wished he could have learned to play it.

Twenty minutes ago he had shown the clip to a young man riding a bike through the park--a teenager with a Yankees hat turned backwards on his head, a seller for all Lance knew--calling him over to him with a discreet nod after circling a couple of times.

"You sellin' that?" the biker said, already calculating an appraisal from the local pawn shop.

"Naw, dude. I just want you to see this." Lance held up the iPod and let one of the earbuds dangle to provide the soundtrack, a static whisper in the stillness.

"*...And Lance Harlan is out live at First Bank Pavilion to give us a glimpse of the Extreme Sports Tour...*"

The Crawlspace

"Wait, let me fast forward past this part..."

"Okay, Rick, Diane, we'll toss it back to you..."

"This is the killer right here..."

"I've been practicing a little bit here...Okay, Ready? Here we go!"

"Ooooh, shit!" The kid on the bike held his hand to his mouth trying to keep his laughter out of earshot of any authorities who may be lurking nearby.

Lance smiled. The kid's laughing fit wasn't very distinct--kind of quiet and subdued--but he still appreciated the sound of it. He liked how they all sounded when they laughed.

"That face," Lance asked, "do you recognize it?"

"Naw, never seen him before. Lemme see that again!"

Out of courtesy, Lance showed it a second time. All the way from the beginning. All the way to the end. It never gets old.

That was twenty minutes ago.

The tingly feeling in his face and hands was gone now and his iPod was turned off. The guitar string was wiped clean and back in his jacket pocket.

Lance looked down at both pieces of the teenager on the ground, smiled and said, "Thank you for teaching me to laugh at myself." And he meant it. And maybe one day he'd find someone who could perfectly imitate that funny little barking sound. And then he'd leave the world alone.

He turned and walked home. Time for a frozen dinner and a beer, and maybe a little TV. But not the local news. He hated watching the news.

The Crawlspace

They fed.

The lucky ones at the front stuffed themselves on the intruder until they were engorged and their silvery exteriors blushed in the color of its unfamiliar blood. The towering thing that invaded their black dwelling was easily overwhelmed by their numbers and their hunger. They had not seen such a creature before. Many of them died in the effort to bring it down, but the reward was a plentiful feast for the quickest ones, a welcome alternative to eating each other as they were accustomed. And there were many tastes for them to enjoy--meaty parts, calcified parts, spongy parts-- but the salty red liquid that seeped from within and bubbled up into their mouths, the sticky, earthy taste of it, filled them with a forbidden satisfaction, and they wanted more.

The carrion had grown cold and they had eaten as much as they could eat when their antennae suddenly shifted toward a faint pounding in the distance. Many of them could sense another intruder, similar to the one they subdued earlier. Towering, smelling of a strange meat. The remaining ones crawled up over their overfed or crushed brothers and sisters and stood at attention, flicking their antennae toward the sound and smell.

In their space, there was no concept of fear, nothing that could intimidate or terrorize them. In fact they only knew how to breed and feed. Thousands of years of simple survival. More luminous than scorpions. Swifter than cockroaches. Unknown to earthly science. And now, bloodthirsty.

The pounding grew louder and the meaty smell grew more pungent. More of them came up from the darkness. Hungry and curious. Bloodthirsty.

And the thousands of them crawled forward as one...

Shawn Braver could smell the ocean for the first time in over a decade, and when the warm, salty air drifted into his lungs as he stood on the edge of Pacific Coast Highway overlooking the beach, he knew the city had already welcomed him back. He hoped his family would do the same.

It was nearly six in the morning and the thin, young Black man had driven all the way from Albuquerque, stopping only for gas, food and thirty-minute catnaps. He had no money to expend on a stay in a motel; in fact, another half a tank and a bag of fries would leave him broke. Home was the only place left. He took a whiff of the ocean air one last time, then hopped in his car and drove. He didn't have far to go.

Shawn had not seen his home since he reluctantly left for college, and when he dropped out to play bass

The Crawlspace

for a rock band that went nowhere, the relationship with his parents became strained. Living the destitute life of a struggling musician kept him out of touch, and he regretted missing those Christmases, birthdays and funerals. Now, out of the band and with nothing left but a smelly, dented Corolla carrying two boxes and three garbage bags full of his worldly possessions, he wanted to make it up to them. How cool would it be, he thought, for Mom and Dad to see their only son standing at the front door after all these years. At least that's what he'd hoped, because all his friends were hundreds of miles away, and he had no "plan B."

Retracing the way by memory, he made it to his childhood home in Redondo Beach almost an hour later. Parking curbside and standing at the crook of the driver's side door, he stared and remembered.

From the outside, the house had changed very little. The old willow tree that scared him when it banged against his bedroom window on windy, rainy nights was gone, but that was the only significant difference he could see. The two-story beach house was still the perfect model of Southern California suburbia, solid and stately but casual. Time may have dulled its warm cream exterior, but not its familiarity. Just looking at the lush, green front lawn triggered the memories of how the grass felt like silk between his toes. He wondered if he would still find his green Moto X bike parked behind the garage door where he had always left it. Shawn brushed back his dreadlocks and smiled. A man can call a lot of places home, but only one is worth coming back to.

As he walked up the concrete walkway to the front door, he fished around on his keychain looking for the house key his mother gave as a symbolic gift the year he left for college. "No matter what happens," she had told him, "you can always come back." That was before she and his father found out he had squandered their tuition money and the wall of anger was built.

He knocked on the front door and waited. He knocked again. He thought about using the key, but wasn't sure if that was the right idea at seven o'clock in the morning. Better to surprise them slowly, he thought.

"Shawn…Shawn, is that you?"

Shawn looked behind him and saw the kindly face of Mr. Collins, still living in the house across the street, still amiable and a touch odd, staring at him like his front porch was an antique shop and Shawn was a precious collectible.

"Well, I'll be doggone! Little Shawn, how are you?" Mr. Collins smiled and extended his hand. "What are you doing out here?"

"Oh…hi, Mr. Collins," Shawn said, shaking his hand, recalling the time he twisted his ankle playing football on the beach with his kids. "Just visiting Mom and Dad for awhile."

"You know, I haven't seen Stan and Jan for over a week," said Collins. "I'm guessing they're on vacation or something, though they never told me they were going anywhere."

The Crawlspace

The two reacquainted themselves, talking about the neighborhood and Albuquerque and some strange infestation in Collins's house, and they parted with Shawn reassuring his chatty, graying neighbor that he had a key and he could wait for his parents to get home. As Collins waved goodbye another memory came to Shawn, one that filled him with trepidation.

His house was fitted with a security alarm shortly before he left for college. He hoped the code was still the same, otherwise he would have to explain to the police why he was breaking and entering into his own house.

He inserted the key in the doorknob and turned it counterclockwise, expecting the warning chirps to fire from within the garage to be followed in exactly 60 seconds by the obnoxious blaring of an alarm loud enough to wake the block and transmitting a silent summons to the Redondo Beach P.D.

Shawn pushed the door open. There were no such noises. The alarm wasn't set.

The inside, lit only by the light of mid-morning, felt fresher and livelier than his boyhood recollections. A new, blue shag carpet covered the living room floor, and the wood tile floor in the entryway was now white marble. It was modernized in his absence, and he didn't mind the changes at all.

And then he heard a faint rustling sound under the floor that moved from one side of the living room to the other, and then fading away.

All throughout the house there were indications of someone living there—dirty dishes in the sink, two cars in the garage, a small TV set in the study (the room that used to be his) turned on for no audience—and yet there was no trace of Stan, Jan or anyone. Shawn could feel his stomach changing colors inside him, and the search for logical explanations began.

If they were on vacation, he thought, Mom sure as hell wouldn't leave the house a mess. Where would they be going in such a hurry? A family emergency? Maybe that was it.

Shawn picked up the phone on the wall of the kitchen and started to dial his mother's cell phone number and then hesitated. How long has it been since his last phone conversation with his mother? Two, three years? Far too long for the woman who gave him life and showed him how to live it to go without hearing her son's voice. A lingering shame wrapped over him as he recalled the ugliness of their last conversation, which was a fair interpretation of the universal parent/child clash of dreams versus reality. At a time of confusion over her and Dad's whereabouts, he wished his mind didn't go there.

His fingers examined the kitchen wall. He didn't know when the wallpaper was removed for a more favorable paint job in eggshell white, but he had never forgotten that tacky, paisley pattern in a palette of soft greens that was once considered the height of home fashion. He recalled a younger image of Jan against the wallpaper, tall and elegant in a sleeveless blouse and clam-digger pants, setting down a plate of lamb chops, sweet potatoes and fresh green beans at his spot on the

The Crawlspace

dining room table, smiling that smile that reminded him every day that he was loved.

He dialed the number having no idea what he would say when she picked up. He thought he heard a song somewhere far away.

He heard four rings, then the simple message of her voicemail. He felt painted into a corner when he heard the tone, but he did his best.

"Hi, Mom. It's me. I came home today. I told you I was coming home...where are you? And where's Dad? Give me a call at your home number as soon as you get this message. I...I really want to talk to you. I miss you. Bye, Mom. Love you."

His heart felt empty as he hung up the phone, still clutching to the belief that he would soon re-establish contact with his parents, but with the same dreadful sense of loss he felt when he got lost on the beach at the age of four...soon wouldn't be soon enough.

Another distant sound was whispering in his head. A faint, dissonant vibration that echoed from somewhere inside the house...familiar but not recognizable. *Mmmm-mmmm...Mmmm-mmmm...Mmmm-mmmm.* He couldn't place it.

And then came the other noise, the one he heard minutes before. The flittering of legs underneath the floor...tiny legs...deep underneath. He put his ear to the kitchen floor. It sounded to him like a gathering of creatures scurrying to points under the foundation, then down. The scurrying sound disappeared, but the other sound above him did not.

Darryl Dawson

Mmmm-mmmm…Mmmm-mmmm…Mmmm-mmmm.

It reminded him of a heartbeat, but not a natural one. And it was coming from upstairs. He was sure of that.

He got up and ran upstairs to the master bedroom. The twin vibrations became clearer to him as he got closer to the nightstand.

He opened the drawer and saw his mother's cell phone glowing and buzzing, signaling a missed call from a number labeled "Home."

The HDTV in the living room was tuned to some bad action movie with more explosions and bloody noses than star power and logical plot points. Shawn was lying on the couch trying to be interested, an empty bowl stained with the remnants of raisin bran and fat-free milk sat on the coffee table in front of him. It was about a quarter after three in the morning, and he couldn't sleep.

Stan and Jan…Dad and Mom…had not called the house, and no one had dropped by. Shawn was out of money and had no means to get more. The food, bland as it was, would last for awhile. His guitars were gone. He was worried shitless about his parents. And about the crawling sounds.

He would hear the occasional subterranean rustling throughout the day, and only now was he beginning to tie it to what Mr. Collins was saying earlier in the day, about the infestation problem he was having. He just

The Crawlspace

mentioned it casually, not saying whether it was rats or termites or whatever. Now it bothered him. He could live with the new TV and the painted walls of the kitchen, but not vermin. He had no tolerance for vermin, having had his fill of them living in scummy, broken-down flats with his bandmates. Cockroaches especially made him ill with fright. But the things he heard crawling beneath his feet sounded too large to be cockroaches or termites, and too quiet to be rats. And how did they get here, to a house and a neighborhood kept so clean?

Maybe that's why Mom and Dad aren't here, he thought with a shudder. Maybe they were driven out.

But their cars are still in the garage…

The crawling started again. Little legs on little things. Faint, distant, but still too close.

Shawn got up and paced around the living room while trying to swallow the lump in his throat. He was beginning to believe that it might not be safe to stay there. He could probably stay in Collins's place if push came to shove, but, at least he had to know what he was dealing with.

Stan had always kept a large MagLite under the kitchen sink in case the power went out, and made sure his son knew where to find it in an emergency. Shawn looked, and it was still there, and it still worked.

He aimed the beam at an area near the laundry room and found the most logical place to start looking for whatever creatures were marching under the house…the crawlspace.

The cramped, concrete-laden basement was an area designed for brief visits—to switch on breakers, check pipes, store Christmas decorations. The darkness and the murky smell were once intimidating to Shawn when he was a boy, and one venture into the dusty underground room led to nightmares of the house collapsing on top of him. As he grew older it became less scary, especially when he discovered a box of his father's old Playboy magazines in the far corner. When his parents were out he would make the crawlspace his retreat, settling down with his flashlight and his Sony Walkman on the cool concrete studying and worshipping the female form. The only bugs he had seen down there were silverfish and garden spiders, and they never interrupted his self-exploration.

But here, hunched over on his hands and knees and fending off the darkness with his flashlight, he felt unnerved. Torn, weathered tarp hung down like dying tree limbs from between the wooden beams in the ceiling. The air felt old, weighted and tepid, and undisturbed by any level of sound. Brushing the dust and cobwebs from his face he followed the MagLite's beam to every corner, listening for the crawling sounds, hearing nothing.

And then he saw what looked like a second door in the far corner next to the box of holiday decorations, opposite the entrance. It wasn't much more than a three-by-three-foot slab of unfinished wood, and there was a hole instead of a doorknob. He tried to remember if he'd ever seen it before and he couldn't recall. He shined the light through the hole and cocked his ear. Nothing.

Those things are probably back here, he assumed, and he almost turned and crawled out of the dingy space to head straight upstairs to the shower, but an unanswered question rooted him to the spot. They are probably back there, but what are *they?* Something he can control? Something best left to an exterminator? Or nothing at all? Perhaps he was feeling the results of long stretches of off and on sleep—some kind of aural hallucination.

And if not...?

There were many times in Shawn's life when his courage would come into question, especially from himself. He sat for a moment wondering if now should be one of those times.

He grabbed the empty doorknob and pulled the door open, and what he saw left him dumbstruck.

The cavern on the other side seemed to be carved out from the earth with spoons, just wide enough to crawl through and descending into an unsettling blackness. A light, pungent smell of dead animals wafted from within that blackness, as did the faint echo of little scratches against the surface from deep and far below.

Shawn could not put a finger on what kept him from turning around and walking out into the safety of the house. Perhaps it was the idea that in his eighteen years of living there he had never seen this passageway, nor had either of his parents made mention of it.

Shawn gathered his breath. What could be down there, what secrets?

Fighting off his instincts, he crawled inside.

The dirt was damp and clammy and sticking to his sweatpants as he crept on his belly along the descending tunnel. He would answer his questions and then leave, he convinced himself; find out, then get out.

He crawled for another ten minutes not thinking of anything more.

There was a point where the walls of the tunnel became wider and taller, allowing Shawn to walk almost upright. He did not know how deep underground he was. The thought of the house falling on top of him grew into an unsteady nausea like it did when he was a boy.

The flashlight's beam came upon something silvery crawling on the ceiling. It moved so fast Shawn could only get a glimpse of it. All of his innards trembled. The beam moved on its own to the floor. He saw a foot.

The shock of that moment made him stumble backwards. His heart beat so fiercely in his chest he was afraid it would cramp up and collapse. As the eye of the flashlight moved along the floor up the length of the leg, revealing another foot, a head, a body, two bodies, the source of the dead animal smell appeared to him as it would in his most excruciating nightmare.

Stan and Jan. The shells of them.

The Crawlspace

Their bodies had been devoured like pomegranates, and within the husks were dozens of long, thin creeping things similar to the one Shawn had discovered earlier. They were the size of rats and resembled wads of spit on white insect legs, sensing the dark world around them with twitching antennae and consuming his parents flesh with locust-like pincers.

Shawn could not find the breath to scream, but soon he would as he felt something crawling up his leg followed by a sharp sting. The flashlight came down on the thing before he willed it, smashing its gelatinous grey innards against his bleeding calf.

As he ran, then crawled on his belly up the dirty tunnel he could hear the crawling sounds again, louder and with the power of hundreds of thousands of tiny legs moving in his direction. He had dropped his flashlight and the darkness was swallowing him up and he wondered what had happened to his home and they were getting closer and oh God Mom and Dad and he felt something crawling on his leg and he was running out of breath and the house is going to fall on him and he felt another sting on the back of his leg, on his side, on the small of his back and he begged the house to fall on him and he could feel them crawling underneath his skin, eating him.

And they fed for a third time.

A TEST OF FAITH

As Helen sat on the edge of the bed knitting and listening to her husband sing gospel songs as he showered, she prayed that this would be the last time, that this would be the day.

They had already had breakfast--Denver omelettes, turkey bacon, toast and orange juice--and after Jim had stuffed the last morsel into his wide face he kissed her on the forehead and muttered his favorite word, "Awesome." She knew the morning meal wasn't anything special, but he was showing his appreciation for it being on time, which was *very* important to him. He could be sweet sometimes.

She was also fully made up and dressed in a modest white cotton nightgown as her husband required. She was quite lovely for being in her late 50's, and Jim made sure that the last thing he saw before he headed out the door was the smiling, doting wife he married and not some "frumpy old broad" just getting up out of bed. *Very* important.

She ended her silent prayer and opened her eyes, looking at the pictures of the two of them and their families on the chest by the door. Above them was a wooden carving of a crying Jesus on the cross. The cross that kept them together.

She smiled and kept her conversation light as the pudgy cab driver emerged from the bathroom, his sullen face relaxed by the warmth and the water pressure, his black chest hairs still clinging to him in slick, swirling formations, a striped towel wrapped below his swollen belly. She watched him dress and primp what little hair he had and splash on the cologne that she disliked but never told him. It was the scent he was wearing the night he knocked out two of her teeth. She stared down at the ghost of a stain on the thin, brown carpet as the harsh, mean fragrance filled the room.

"Did you need anything from the store?" she asked, squeezing her hands together.

"Mmmh," Jim replied with a dismissive shake of his head. She looked at him through the dresser mirror's reflection as he adjusted his tie beneath his meaty jowl.

"Well--I--was planning on going to the store and I--I wanted to make sure I didn't miss anything you might need."

Jim continued to stare at the mirror, and then a cool, hateful smile slithered across his face. "Do you still wish I was dead?" he said.

She didn't expect him to say that, but she answered him quickly and with as much conviction as she could fake. "No, honey! No, that's silly!" Her eyes found the cross on the wall again and saw the wooden face of her Savior twisted in a soundless, scornful moan.

The Crawlspace

He turned to her as his lips sagged like a curtain. "Do you *still* wish I was *dead?*" he asked again.

The flaming memory of what he was referring to burned through the filter of her mind. The notes. The little notes she would write on the computer to empty the pain from her soul. The little notes she never shared with anyone until Jim found them somehow and smashed every component of the desktop into irreparable junk. How angry he was. How it hurt. It was seven months ago. Very important not to do that again. *Very* important.

"Well?" he scowled. *"Do you?"*

She searched her mouth for moisture. The part of the morning she hated was coming, when he would perform the ritual—the new element of his morning routine added just two days after shattering the computer--the demonstration of his divine faith and his wicked will.

She stared straight at him, the oily sheen on his forehead, the slow stab of his arrogant eyes with pupils the color of a toad's skin. "No," she shuddered.

Then she sat, silent and obedient, knowing what was coming, wishing today it would be different, dreading what would happen if it was so.

Jim took out his keys and unlocked a small safe next to the nightstand, and from it he pulled his bible and his revolver and sat them down beside him on the bed. The dark ice of his stare prompted her, and she turned to sit next to him. She gently took his hands in hers and they bowed their heads. In a voice low and respectful he recited the 23rd Psalm from memory and improvised the rest. They both said "Amen," and Jim reached for his pistol.

She had seen this so many times and yet each time felt like the first. A heavy ball grew in her throat and her eyes weighted with fear.

He checked the chamber to make sure it was loaded with a single round as it always was when he went to bed the night before, and it was. He closed the revolver and spun the chambers. "Glory to God," he said with a devilish smile, looking straight into her eyes.

She hated that look. That harsh, mean look. She squeezed her eyes shut.

Jim put the barrel between his teeth and pulled the trigger.

She opened her eyes again. Again, like the seven months of mornings the scene was the same. The walls were white and the room was quiet.

Jim, unshaken and confident, put his gun and bible back where he would always find it and locked the safe door. He checked his watch and kissed his wife on the cheek with a broad smile as he stood up from the bed. "Keep wishing," he whispered. Humming another gospel song, he went off to work.

She listened for the door to shut and said her own prayer for strength and understanding. The sounds of Jim's car starting up and driving away rumbled from behind the window, which was shielded by a blue curtain with sword-like diamond patterns. She shut her eyes and whispered another prayer for forgiveness.

The Crawlspace

She still wished he was dead. She could write it down here, in a place where he would never find it. She still wished he was dead.

Twenty-eight years she's been with Jim. Twenty-eight years of a horrible marriage, with the last seven months being the most unbearable, seven months of mornings with the same dull click, the same victorious walk, and the same wait for tomorrow, loathing him, fearing him, waiting for God to allow him one mistake. She still wished he was dead. And it will come, she thought. Soon, if not tomorrow. Soon. Soon.

She started planning her errands for the day. The supermarket. The mall. The locksmith.

Jim had performed his little trick for her every day for another week (*Click.* Soon, Soon...). Looking more closely at his gun, she was finally able to figure out how he did it--the little notch on the front of the chamber, how it had to be positioned just right. The simplicity of it made her react with a silent chuckle of embarrassment...or maybe it was relief. She had just locked it up again when she heard his car pulling up into the driveway hours earlier than normal. He was coming home sick, probably those stomach pains he was complaining about yesterday. She quickly stowed the gardening gloves and the sauce brush under the bed.

"Where's the goddamn Pepto?" Jim grumbled as he limped through the front door clutching his belly.

His wife came quickly into the kitchen. "What's wrong?" she said. "Oh, honey, are you sick?" The concern in her voice was real. He looked to be in a lot of pain.

"Pepto! The *Pepto*, goddamit!" he yelled, as though he were expecting it arranged on a dinner platter the moment he entered. She ran back to the master bathroom and retrieved his stomach medicine.

What would happen if he drank this? Would it cancel everything out? Would I have to start over? "C'mon, honey, lie down for a while."

Jim took a large, unmeasured swig from the pink bottle and followed her into the bedroom. He plopped down on the bed with a groan, not bothering to undress.

"Is there anything else I can get you?" she asked. *Did he see anything? He didn't look under the bed, did he?*

He shook his head. She sat next to him on the bed stroking his forehead, mothering him. *If it was enough for a rat, would it be enough...*

"You're not trying to poison me, are you?"

Jim's innocent remark sent an icy jolt through her heart. She kept her composure and didn't reply.

"Naw, you wouldn't," he figured. "You're not that type. You're a good woman, a Christian woman. You like to dream of things, wish for things, but you never act on them. You just wish I was dead, but you don't have the guts to kill me. You're a coward."

The Crawlspace

"Jim," she said, "you really shouldn't think those things."

"Don't tell me what to think!" he yelled. "Love! Honor! And obey!"

And for a moment there was nothing but the angry lunacy of his stare and the trembling inside and the icy feeling. She couldn't look at him. She looked up at the wooden cross again and the agonized face crowned with thorns and the trembling didn't go away. She couldn't look at Jesus either.

He reached into his pocket and pulled out his keys and sat up, wheezing a pained laugh, and weakly made his way to the safe.

She couldn't understand why she felt the same fear as he opened the safe. She had a key made for herself. The curtain had already been lifted on his trick. There would be no surprise this time, no anticipation, no wonder. There was no "Soon..." anymore. And yet the crushing fear of him was no different now that it was over the last seven months.

What if it wasn't enough? Maybe it'll take a little while longer...it's just a little bit a day. But what if it doesn't work? What if he pulls through and he figures it out? What will he do to me? Jesus, what will he do?

Jim read the 23rd Psalm and put the barrel in his mouth.

Can he see it? Can he see it on the barrel? Oh, Jesus, my Lord...

Click.

"You see, baby?" Jim said, shaking and smiling vacantly. "It ain't gonna work. You can wish all you want, it ain't gonna work. God has a plan for me." He licked his lips. "Does God have a plan for you?" And he pointed his gun at her head.

Her eyes widened and took in the full measure of the death side of the gun. She couldn't run. She couldn't see the notch on the chamber.

Jim shook stiffly, uncontrollably. "Open wide, baby! It's your turn!" His finger squeezed. She could feel herself sinking into the bed.

Click.

He collapsed to the floor, convulsing and gasping for the few minutes he had left.

Helen took the gardening gloves from under the bed when he was done and carefully removed the gun from his hand. It was important that he didn't make a mess. *Very* important.

Trick

We don't like Halloween, Gus and I. It's a day for sick people.

If I didn't have to buy candy for you little bastards I damn sure wouldn't. I only do it for Gus's sake. Hell, he probably hates Halloween even more than I do, but every year around the first of October he shows up and starts screaming like hell, like he did on the night he died, all high and screechy, every night until Halloween was over, every year.

And you think I'm a mean old lady getting stir crazy living by myself in this old house! Don't think I don't get wind of what you little shits call me: "mean old Mrs. Landry, the fat old bag, the crazy lady." Well, I guess if somebody killed *your* cat, *your* best friend, you'd probably end up a little pissed off at the world, too, wouldn't you?

I loved Gus. He was the only friend I ever had. We just kind of *found* each other after my husband, That-Cheating-Son-of-a-Bitch, divorced me (don't get me started). Actually, it wasn't long after we separated that this big, charcoal-grey furball came tiptoeing around my front yard, and what he was looking for I don't know. At first I wanted to shoo him away, but there was something about him. He just looked up at me with those eyes and I let him in. Never heard anything around the neighborhood about a lost cat so I just adopted the little sweetie. He was a perfect little cat, more kind, more loving than any man I ever met for sure. And did I spoil him rotten. Sometimes I can still feel him curled up on my lap, purring his little heart out.

And I still remember that morning after Halloween I found him on the side of my house next to an open can of tuna with an arrow through his chest.

You murdered him. You sick, little kids with your sick, cruel little minds and your devil costumes...you murdered him. Why?

Because I wouldn't give you candy?

You litter my house with toilet paper and rotten eggs, you put a goddamn stink bomb in my garage...for *candy?* You kill my best friend...for *candy?*

All right, I've got your damn candy. Lots of it. Big, gooey chocolate bars...all for you, just like last year. Oh, you remember last year, don't you?

Tell me, did they ever figure out what happened to Corey, the only kid who had the nerve to come trick-or-treating at my house? The one who got his eyes scratched out? Probably just some wild animal, huh? Some coyote came up out of nowhere and wiped

The Crawlspace

its claws on his face and blinded him, is that how you think it happened?

You're all stupid. You have no idea. Gus knows the real story. And he'll tell you…sure as hell. He'll jump right up on your little vampire faces and tell you everything you need to know. Damn straight!

Gus and I, we don't care much for Halloween, but we'll play along with you. If you decide to come up to "mean old Mrs. Landry's house," you'll find a big bowl of candy sitting on the front porch. Take as many as you want, I don't mind. I'll be inside looking out from the upstairs window.

There…you hear him screaming? It's okay, Gussie-Gussie. We'll have some company soon.

I Scream, You Scream

Whenever the subject comes up I always lie. Not that I feel any particular kind of shame about what really happened (though it is hard to talk about), but sometimes a short, quick explanation works better than the truth. If you looked at my right hand and I told you I had an accident with a power tool or I got it caught in a garbage disposal when I was young, it would make sense to you, wouldn't it?

But that's not true. Yes, I did lose my finger years ago, but the story isn't that simple.

It's hard to believe what dangerous times we lived in when my generation was little; no car seats, no bike helmets, no pool fences. How the hell did we all survive? Maybe we were just smarter.

I remember the ice cream trucks, those crawling oil-burners that crept up and down the streets of Torrance, California, filling the air with jangly, obnoxious music and selling cheap confections to crowds of unsupervised kids. They used to roam my neighborhood two or three at a time, and everyone considered them harmless, and for the most part they were. When I was a kid and playing football in the street with my friends (I pretended I was O.J. Simpson, because I thought he was better than whoever was the running back for the Rams), that dissonant noise coming down our street was like Pan's flute. God knows how much allowance money we burned on Bomb Pops, Fudgesicles and Wacky Packs.

One truck in particular was called "Big Blue," a boxy, Chevy utility van covered in ghoulish blue house paint, slightly darker than the face of a Blue Meanie in *Yellow Submarine*. "Big Blue" wasn't the nickname we gave it; that name was scrawled across the front in canary-yellow block letters. Most ice cream trucks would be decorated with rough drawings of Bugs Bunny and Superman, but not this one. It was beyond plain; it looked displaced and unhappy like an ex-con canvassing the county fair in a mascot costume. Of course, the kids didn't care how it looked as long as it had plenty of teeth-rotting treats for us to buy.

But the thing is, the driver looked as bad as the van he drove. Strange-looking motherfucker. He was probably in his mid-thirties and not-too-thin. The top of his head was shiny bald but he had a ring of rusty brown hair that grew out just above his ears and ended in a lazy drape across his shoulder. His face was small and pinched, his lower lip sticking up in a permanent, angry pout, and the corner of his left eye was always red as if it were constantly poked with a popsicle stick, or maybe diseased. I don't remember him wearing anything other than a tight-fitting, oily white tank top and a dirty pair of grey Dickies. And for an ice cream truck driver he never smiled much. He wasn't mean or grouchy, but he was far from the Good Humor Man, serving our goodies like it was some cruel fate he had

The Crawlspace

to endure. All the kids called him Mr. Pigface, but I guarantee you no-one ever called him by that name within his earshot.

There was always some gnawing sensation in my gut whenever I saw the guy, and it wasn't just his appearance. I think I was born with a built-in divining rod that senses the evil in people. Every kid nowadays has to learn the whole "stranger-danger" routine (I brought my daughter up the same way), but for me, a lot of that was just instinct. With some people, I just knew, and with Pigface, his demeanor just put me on edge. Not enough to avoid doing business with him, though. I handed him a sweaty, crinkly dollar bill, he handed me a candy bar and a couple of packs of baseball cards, and that was it. We never exchanged more words than were necessary, and that was fine with me.

The last meaningful conversation we had was when I was ten years old, the day it happened.

School was maybe a mile and a half from my front door, but I always took the quick route down the edge of the canal and through one long, filthy back alley behind a mobile home park. A lot of things went on in that alley that I didn't ask my mom about, but I wasn't afraid to go through it, even though most of my peers stayed away for being grossed out. I just knew not to touch anything that was on the ground, not even the porno mags.

I was walking home late, close to four in the afternoon, after serving detention (Got into a fight with some smart-ass kid who called me a nigger and I nearly put his eye out). I was all by myself, and if there was anybody watching me, they couldn't save me.

I could hear the jangling song of the ice cream truck coming up from behind me, a tinny variation of "Sailing, Sailing, Over The Bounding Main" in an endless loop, and I knew it was Big Blue. I didn't look up, just stared at my Keds pounding the dirty sidewalk. The ugly blue van roared up past me and pulled over a few yards away.

I could hear Pigface yelling something to me over the din of the music. "Hey, kid! Want some free ice cream?" His voice had the snappy, authoritative drawl of a Texan.

If the situation was different and I was a little older and smarter, I would have kept on walking. But it was a long day and I had about a mile of walking to do before I could grab a cold glass of milk or make myself a sandwich. I stopped. Free? Shit.

"What's your name, kid?"

"Dooley," I said. Pops came up with that nickname. Thanks, Pops. Saved me a lifetime of saying and writing out "Deuteronomy Jones," the name on my birth certificate.

Pigface seemed to be in an uncharacteristically good mood as he motioned me over to the window. I could see flies buzzing around behind him and a little smudge on the window ledge that I thought was chocolate at first, but looked a little redder as I got nearer.

The Crawlspace

He handed me a single scoop of grayish vanilla ice cream on a sugar cone. "It's my own special recipe," he bragged. "Try it! Tell me what you think."

It was a weird, unappetizing ice cream cone, the color of a dirty mop. I saw chunks of things in it that didn't look like nuts or chocolate chips or anything that could naturally mix with ice cream. "What's in it?" I asked.

"Taste it!"

I looked again at the thing, trying to understand why an ice cream cone would make me feel the way I did when I was finishing off my asparagus from my dinner plate. Scrunching my nose I gave it a taste. I tasted vanilla. I tasted the chunks, which had a flavor that reminded me of raw bacon, salty and unclean. I held it back and took a look at the sickly-grey scoop and thought I saw something that looked like the tip of a small, dead finger.

"I don't like it," I said, trying not to retch all over his van.

"You don't? Well, give it back, then. Don't throw it on the ground! Hand it back!"

I would have preferred to toss the awful thing on the ground, but anything to get it out of my hands and keep it from dripping on my fingers. I reached up to hand the cone back to him and he grabbed my wrist, squeezing it tight, pulling my arm into the van. I saw him grab a pair of pruning shears from the front pocket of his overalls.

Darryl Dawson

"You wanna know what's in it?" hissed Pigface with a hint of a smile. "You! That's what's in it!"

I screamed once, and then as I felt the crunch on my right index finger I screamed again, much louder.

Of course I lied to my parents about it. When you're a kid, you learn to be a good liar. I think it's part of the natural process of growing up, kind of like an exercise for your imagination.

I stuck with the same lie when we went to the police. The school janitor did it, I said, and I didn't know why he would attack me. I had only seen him at school a couple of times but I did a good enough job of describing his physical appearance that the cops were able to make an arrest. Turns out he was kind of a wack job; he actually believed he did it, thinking he might have been on what we used to call "angel dust" at the time. It would have been safe bet that the dude was always on "angel dust." He represented himself in court. Somehow they pinned him to another kid in a different neighborhood who lost a finger and the drugged-out janitor didn't even argue.

Mom, Pops, and the entire community had no idea who really chopped off my finger. I was pulled out of school and we moved to San Diego in a week. And that janitor went to prison.

I didn't know Pigface, but I knew he had power. He had more control over everything than any cops, teachers or parents, mine included. After he snipped off my finger and sucked the blood out of the wounded end as I screamed, he told me to shut up and not tell

The Crawlspace

anyone, that he would find me if I did and cut off more fingers, then my ears, then my balls...and he'd keep coming back until there was nothing left of me. And then he hopped into the driver's seat and drove away. *Sailing, sailing, over the bounding main...*

I thought about him all the way to San Diego and then I stopped thinking about him. Went to school. Graduated college and got married. Learned that the guy I wrongly sent to prison was murdered there. Saw my baby girl born. Got a job as a firefighter. Cringed whenever I heard an ice cream truck roll by.

After surviving all that Y2K nonsense my daughter left San Diego to go to college in Colorado, and she came back in a casket. She drove drunk. I blamed myself. I watched my wife lose her battle with breast cancer, then a few years later Pops would die and then Momma a few years after that. And in all that time I did a lot of drinking (enough to cost me my job), and every drink told me *It's okay, Dooley, ole buddy. He's not coming after you.* Every sip tried to convince me, but it didn't matter.

Because every now and then I would look down at the stump next to the middle finger on my right hand, and always be reminded.

Sailing, sailing, over the bounding main...

I don't know what brought me back to Torrance. Maybe the need for a weekend getaway in a familiar location, maybe another lead in my search for a second chance. I guess I just fell victim to those nostalgic

Darryl Dawson

pangs we all feel when those childhood ghosts appear and touch you on the shoulder.

San Diego is a beautiful place, and spending most of my life there was more than anyone could ask for. But we all get one home, and mine is in that spacious, racially-mixed suburb ten minutes from the beach. And isn't it only right that the place you spent playing in the street with your friends, head-faking and escaping the secondary like O.J. on your way to an improvised end zone, should be the only place you can truly call home?

I haven't forgotten what happened there and it still frightens me. But there was nine years of good. So I took the drive and puttered around for a couple of days, just to see how everything looked after almost forty years.

I cruised around the neighborhood. All the postmodern houses that gave my street a surreal, early-60's TV sitcom atmosphere were still standing, most with new paint jobs, better lawns and satellite dishes perched on their fireproof-shingled roofs. The house I grew up in now belongs to someone else; I didn't want to know who lives there now, it didn't matter to me.

I drove around a few blocks, twisting and turning along the maze of streets. It was 4:00 in the afternoon in October and there were no kids playing football or anything in the street. I saw an old man watering his lawn...

And I froze, and nearly hit the brakes.

I drove to the end of the street, turned around and parked at a house a dozen yards away to get a better

The Crawlspace

look at the guy. He was in his late sixties, maybe seventies, a little on the thin side with an awkward paunch that jutted over his denim shorts and made his faded blue t-shirt fit too tight. He was bald, completely, with age spots sprinkled on the top of his head. He wore a patch over his left eye. His face was small, scrunched up, his lower lip forced upward in a permanent, angry pout.

It was Mr. Pigface. No doubt in my mind. And he was living in my neighborhood.

As I watched him turn off his garden hose and go back into his house, my fear gave way to rage. I had nine good years here. Nine years.

Why is he living here, where my childhood lives? What gives him the goddamn right?

I drove to the nearest Kmart (where Pops used to buy my toys and his hardware) and drove straight back to that house while I still remembered where it was. Two blocks away from what used to be my front door. Maybe it was his house all along, I don't know. But just the fact that he lived there...it made me sad. It made me boil over.

I knocked. Waited, knocked again. And then I began to think, what's the point? Will standing face-to-face with him make all the pain go away? Change my life? Make my finger grow back?

I heard footsteps and my heart stuttered. The door opened a crack, held taut against a chain. I saw only a portion of his face, and that was all I needed to see to convince me that this was the ice cream man the kids called Pigface, the only person in this world who knows the truth about my mutilation. "Yeah?" he grumbled.

"Hello...I, ah..." What should I say? What *can* be said? "I...wanted to talk to you about..."

"I don't wanna buy nothin' from nobody," he muttered as he shut the door.

"*...about your ice cream recipe!*" I blurted out. I stood there for a moment thinking he probably doesn't remember, and maybe that would be best for both of us. As I turned to walk away the door popped open.

Pigface had a look of puzzled anger. "Who are you?" he said.

I wanted to drop the whole thing and drive back to San Diego, but something wouldn't let me. "I used to live in this neighborhood," I said. "A couple of streets down."

He shut the door again, but this time to unhook the security chain and open the door wider. Standing in the doorway, a foot shorter than me but still with that menacing presence, he stared at me as if he were trying to open up my skull like a book and read my thoughts. Even the eye buried beneath his patch seemed to burn a hole through me.

"C'mon in," he said.

I asked myself again, what's the point? What would it prove? I couldn't answer, but then I couldn't answer anything. I felt like a rat was clawing around inside my stomach. I went back up the steps of his porch and followed him in.

The Crawlspace

The inside of his house was decorated with paintings and photographs of war--dive-bombing planes, square-jawed soldiers, tanks and tattered flags--mostly World War II and Vietnam. Over the brick mantle was a solid metal coat-of-arms, with a black-and-white photo of a smiling John Wayne to its right. The furniture was decades old and worn thin in spots, junk to rest of the world, and the air smelled as dusty and ancient as the furniture. The TV set--working but far from modern--was tuned to one of the sports channels. All the curtains and blinds were drawn, and even the natural daylight that crept in couldn't soften the coffin-like atmosphere of the house.

Pigface asked me sit down and I did, on the sofa. "So, what's your name?" he said as he sat upright on the recliner.

I almost said "Dooley" but kept quiet. Given the circumstances it would probably be best if he didn't know my name, even if he doesn't remember me. "Jim," I said.

"Well, Jim," Pigface said in an older, scratchier Texas accent, "can I getcha a beer? A glass of water?"

"No, thanks."

He paused. What passed for a smile ebbed into a look of mild concern. "I heard you mention something about ice cream," he said.

I looked down at my hands, making sure he couldn't see them. "Yes."

"I used to make my own ice cream a long time ago," he reflected. "It was a family tradition. My daddy taught me how to put all kinds'a flavors into it. Sometimes I'd make stuff up and just put in whatever the hell was lyin' around. Cut grass, dandelions, fresh leaves, hamburger. Anything. I remember one time I found a dead squirrel in the driveway, and sure 'nuff I cleaned that little bastard up and dropped him right in with the milk and ice and everything. Nobody else liked it, but I did. It was like nothing I ever ate before. When Daddy and I went huntin' and caught ourselves a deer, I'd break off a whole leg, chop it up and drop it in." Pigface closed his eyes. "Man, that was good ice cream! It tasted like...triumph. Like victory. It made you *feel* good, y'know what I mean?"

I could only stare at him as he told his gruesome story. Squirrels, deer...then what? When did he eat his first human?

Pigface got up from his chair and walked into the kitchen. "Y'know, Jim, I'm kinda glad you're here," he said. "There's this big, heavy box in the garage I need help movin' into the house. Nothin' fragile, just stuff I need for the house. I'd do it myself but my back is all shot to hell. You think you can help me with that?"

I hesitated. How nice this old man was, how cordial. Did he know who I was, and why I was here? "You didn't tell me your name," I said.

"I sure would appreciate it," he continued, ignoring me. "You don't need to go far, just from the garage to the living room would be just fine. I can pay ya back with a beer!"

I stood up. If it was going to happen, it had to happen now. There might never be another opportunity. I

The Crawlspace

agreed to help him, and he told me where the garage was.

Even with the light on, the garage was darker than the house, and just a bit colder. I looked around for the "box" he was talking about, and couldn't find it.

What I did find was several sizes of circular saws and hacksaws hanging from the walls. A large workbench stood to the side with a leather apron and a pair of plastic goggles lying on top of it. To its left was a rolled up dark green tarp, two small hatchets and several large bottles of bleach. And all these things were impeccably, disturbingly clean. And then I saw the freezer.

Why I felt the need to look inside the freezer I don't know to this day. I understood what kind of monster I was dealing with, but even as that image of that sick ice cream truck driver sucking the blood from my severed finger flashed in my head, I couldn't grasp what kind of evil this man was capable of. My heart pumped so hard it felt like it was growing. I had to see...Open the lid and see...

Inside the freezer were limbs. Human arms and legs. Frozen, dead limbs.

I felt a cold, hard stab in my side and I leaped back and buckled from the pain.

Pigface was holding a kitchen knife that bled at its tip. He stabbed me again, this time in my face, an inch short of my eye and dragging down my cheek.

"I remember you!" Another stab in the gut, but not too deep.

Darryl Dawson

He glared at me with that ugly, demonic expression that kept me awake on many nights until the sneer on his lips bent upward in a meaty, crooked smile and he cackled, "I love Black people! They taste so damn *good!*" He laughed at my pain, again.

The knife left several deep gashes in my arm as I deflected his attacks away. All I had to defend myself with was the pruning shears I had just bought, sitting in my back pocket.

He lunged again, aiming for my stomach, and I grabbed his wrist and kicked him hard between the legs. He crumpled to the concrete floor and I knelt on top of him with my knee against his head. I bent his arm back until he was in too much pain to hold the knife anymore, and it dropped to the ground.

And there they were. His fingers. His old, wormy little fingers, reaching up to the sky for mercy.

I grabbed the pruning shears from my pocket and put them against his index finger. I saw my own stump and felt the crunch, felt the pain all over again, felt the rage--too much rage to make a sound. I squeezed and chopped off his finger.

Then his middle finger. Then his third. Then his pinky.

He made a kind of wheezing, whimpering sound, but he didn't scream much. That disappointed me. I left him there, bleeding.

I was able to drive myself to the hospital. Yes, I got stabbed, I told them. No big deal. Just a little

The Crawlspace

disagreement between friends. I don't want to press charges. They bought it.

The scars don't really bother me, not even the old one anymore. I can look at it and not feel like something horrible was chasing me to the bitter end. I don't reflect on all the family I've lost and all the things I wish I could have said. That's over now. That and the booze--done. I just feel a whole helluva lot better now.

So much so that I've moved back to Torrance, right back where I started. Found a respectable apartment and a nice, quiet job at the library. The pay's okay but these days a little extra income never hurts, so I got a side job.

I was surprised to see how little it costs to rent one of those vans. Not much to operate, either. You order as much as you need and you keep the profits. And the music...well, you get used to it after a while. Come to think of it, after listening to it a few thousand times, it's beginning to sound kinda nice.

Sailing, sailing, over the bounding main...

Isn't that a pretty melody? I wonder what Mr. Pigface thinks of it every time I drive down his street.

THE PROPER TECHNIQUE

It was not so much a rehearsal as it was a briefing. With the last of the fifty dollar checks and free tickets handed out to his "subjects", Pervis Clay, Comedy Hypnotist, had one final warning before allowing the five community theatre actors to disperse from the orchestra pit of the otherwise empty theatre. "Alright, people," the jovial, portly man declared in his booming Brooklyn accent, "this is the last time I'm gonna tell you, so let's review. Number one?"

"Not a word of this to anyone!" the young group repeated in chorus, except for one.

"Number two?"

"Do exactly as you say!"

"And number three, if you don't show up I will what?"

"Hunt us down!" The group giggled at the final exaggerated command, but one long-haired man, dressed in baggy shorts and a black shirt advertising a rock band nobody had heard of, failed to see the humor in any of it.

"Damn right I will!" Pervis responded, smiling but serious. "Thank you very much for your participation, and I guarantee I'll make stars out of all of you!" The actors then headed up the aisles to the theatre exit with nervous excitement. The long-haired man stayed behind.

Pervis remained seated at the edge of the stage, stuffing his checkbook into the pocket of his Nike warm-up jacket, satisfied with the delivery of his waiver of liability pep talk. It was a speech he had delivered hundreds of times in dozens of towns from Vegas to Atlantic City, and every time sounded good to him, because it meant the money wasn't far behind.

The long-haired man got up from his aisle seat and approached the stage, hands in his pockets, with a look on his bearded face that fell somewhere between contempt and amusement. "You sound like quite the entertainer," he said in a British accent, staring up at the chubby, casually-dressed man standing above him.

"Been doing it for years," Pervis replied. "Used to be strictly stand-up until I put the hypnotism thing in my act."

"The 'hypnotism thing'?"

"Yeah, everybody's gotta have an angle, right?" Pervis pulled a pack of cigarettes from the same pocket where his checkbook was stowed. "What was your name again?"

"There's no smoking in the theatre," the long-haired man said matter-of-factly. "And my name is James."

Pervis gave him an odd look and stuffed the pack back into his jacket. "My bad, pal."

The Crawlspace

"So where does someone like you acquire the knowledge of the application of hypnotherapy?"

"Hypnotherapy?" Pervis laughed. "Listen, guy, what I do up here ain't got nothing to do with therapy! Pornography, maybe, but therapy? Absolutely not!"

James chuckled. "How true, Mr. Clay, how true! And said without a drop of shame! That's so admirable."

Pervis had a feeling the conversation was leading in a direction he didn't want to go. He sat down at the edge of the stage to get a closer look at the scruffy young man with the attitude. "What's the matter, you getting cold feet? Listen, I promise whatever you do, you'll be fully clothed…"

"Not at all, Mr. Clay…"

"…And can you call me Pervis, alright? I'm not one of your drama teachers."

James had little reaction to the personal jab. "I'm sorry, Pervis. I'm just a bit curious about your background, is all."

"You wanna know about my background? Alright, kid. Which version do you want?"

He nudged his pudgy body off the stage foot, stretching one leg to the floor and allowing the rest of him to slump behind it like a bag of fertilizer falling off a flatbed. He now stood close enough to strangle James, but his patience hadn't been broken just yet.

"There's the version in my press release," Pervis continued, "that's the one you're probably familiar with. The one that explains how I acquired my unique skills from the teachings of an ancient Middle Eastern mystic in exchange for never publicly revealing his name."

"Right," James smiled. "And the other version?"

"That's the one I just got finished discussing with you Oscar-winners-in-training. I've been a professional comedian for as long as you've been alive, and I'll be honest with you, I wasn't exactly Jerry Seinfeld. I've taken everything an audience has to give, but I never quit. Now, after twenty years in show business, I finally found an act that works. To make it work the way I want to requires a bit of, eh...preparation. I take out an ad in the college paper, you and your buddies answer, we make a deal, we perform, I get paid, you get paid, and everybody walks out happy. So what's the matter? Something bother you about my act?"

James glanced at the hypno-comic's running shoes. "It does more than bother me, Pervis. It insults me."

Pervis stared at the young man with the airy, cockney twang with bemusement.

"I should probably make you familiar with *my* background," James said, walking back to a front row seat. "Do you know who James Braid is?"

"Doesn't ring a bell."

"Of course not. Many consider him the father of modern hypnotism. Gave it its name, matter of fact. See, James Braid wasn't an entertainer like you, he was a doctor. He believed that hypnotism should be used to heal people, not humiliate them."

"So what does that have to do with you?"

The Crawlspace

"Dr. Braid was my great-great grandfather."

Pervis cocked his head like a dog trying to make sense of a strange whistle. "Wait a minute! I think I feel a 'whoop-dee-fucking-doo' coming on. I can almost feel it...Nope, I think I missed it."

James laughed quietly, being careful not to give Pervis too much credit for a good comeback. "You're very good at making a mockery of things. It's a shame you were such a lousy comedian."

The humor melted from Pervis's face. Now *he* was insulted.

James went on, "And now you think a little backstage bribery and a traveling dog and pony show make you a hypnotist? I don't think so, mister. You don't have the technique. You need a little preparation to make strangers do your bidding. I don't."

Pervis stared into the young man's eyes.

"I know your mind from the inside out," James said, softening his voice. "I know every button to push..."

"All right," Pervis said. "You know that check I handed to you a few minutes ago? Well, you can hand it right back 'cause there's no way you're getting on stage with me tonight!"

"You needn't be afraid of me, Pervis."

"Afraid of *you?* I ain't afraid of a goddamn thing! Now give me back my money or you're gonna be afraid of me!"

"You needn't be afraid of me, Pervis." James's voice was soothing, washing over Pervis and short-circuiting his need for argument. The Englishman would repeat the phrase five more times, quieter each time until it was barely above a whisper. For Pervis, the house lights were falling out of focus behind James and all he could see was the calm, angelic visage of the drama student, who was now whispering to him in a language that only his subconscious could interpret. His chubby body felt feathery and his eyes were tired and ready to shut. He stood still in his confused, blissful state until he heard…

"Three."

He stumbled as he awakened, catching himself and sucking in a startled breath. He looked around at the theater and forgot, just for a moment, what it was, where it was and why he was there.

James was holding him up by the shoulder. "Are you all right?"

Pervis had a foggy recollection of the long-haired young man, a sense of *déjà vu* over an event that hadn't happened yet in his life. He didn't remember his name, or the conversation they had minutes ago. "Yeah, uh… I'm fine," he weakly replied.

"Poor guy, you've had a long day," James suggested. "You should probably head back to the hotel and get some rest."

Pervis said nothing, only staring at him and trying to remember.

James walked up the aisle and toward the exit. "So I'll see you tonight, then?"

The Crawlspace

After a mediocre set from a local comic, Pervis came out onstage to a respectable round of applause. The first part of his act went as though he and his set-ups had gone through weeks of rehearsal. One of them pretended to sneeze every time he heard his own name, another performed lewd acts on a folding chair while another was convinced that chair was a boyfriend who was cheating on her. Pervis, a picture of campy supernatural authority in his shiny, fake turban, punctuated his charade of hypnotic suggestion with improvised commentary. The crowd was laughing in all the right places. He was a hit yet again.

For the second part of his act he sent the first three actors (perfectly feigning a sudden reattachment to reality) back into the audience and chose two more from their seats in the first row, with James being one of them, and they took their place on the stage.

Pervis looked at James as he took his seat, the game-show-host expression on his face not changing, but feeling a little unnerved and not knowing why. He had no reason not to trust the long-haired fellow, but he couldn't and didn't. Maybe it was his Christ-like presence, the stern, commanding look in his olive-green eyes. In the seconds he stared at James, he tried to remember a conversation he had with him, if he had any conversation.

James was saying something under his breath that made him remember a distant, sketchy pattern that formed somewhere in the back of his brain. Pervis felt tired enough to take a nap right there on the stage, but he couldn't bring himself to do it. Wouldn't be professional, he thought, or tried to think. He could hear a young, British voice counting to three, and on the third count a strange chill washed over him, making him turn away from the audience and clear his throat. Fighting off his grogginess, he continued.

"Everybody comfortable? Good, because you all look like you could use a little *SLEEP*!" Pervis then waved his hand in front of their faces and made a meaningless whooshing sound, and the three actors pretended to sleep.

"You are now in my zone," Pervis commanded, "and you will do exactly as I say without hesitation or shame. I will control your thoughts, your movements and your desires for the amusement of all these lovely people…"

He thought he heard that voice again, fluttering against his eardrum from the inside and telling him… something?…nothing? He stopped and cleared his throat again.

"Holy shit, folks, you're killing me with this dry weather! This town should be called Easy Bake!" The laughter he heard was tinged with nervousness. Something was really burning in his throat. He coughed into his hand, and a second time louder.

Something was in his throat, choking him. He coughed like a cannon, bellowing, heaving and bending at his waist until something large and slimy came up from his mouth and settled in his closed hand. "Oh, Jeez Louise!" he wheezed as his coughing fit stopped. "Whoo, that's it. No more crack before breakfast!" He couldn't laugh along with the spectators on this one. His head ached too much.

The Crawlspace

He opened his hand and saw a small lizard licking the expelled droplets of blood from his palm. It crawled over the crotch of his thumb and into his shirt sleeve.

Pervis gasped and flicked his arm wildly as he felt the blood-stained gecko crawling under his tuxedo shirt and disappearing past his shoulder. Someone was whispering to him again, and though he couldn't quite understand what the voice was saying he could feel it somehow, bouncing off his inner ears, guiding him somewhere. He found himself in a surreal, familiar place…an imitation of his concept of reality, a dream that wasn't his.

The audience was laughing. Pervis turned his pudgy, sweating face toward the darkness of the theatre, the source of the laughter. This was not the compliant response of a comedian's audience, but more cruel and sadistic. "What's so funny?" he said under his breath. The laughter grew louder.

He looked around and saw his two subjects still seated in "sleep" mode. The act! He had to keep going, keep the show on track. Another whisper.

He forgot what he was supposed to do next. He forgot how to improvise. The derisive laughter grew to the point of screams, out of control. He could feel the blood rushing up his neck to the rhythm of his pounding heart, a new kind of nausea. Sweat coated his face and dripped down into his unblinking eyes, painting them a stinging red as they darted in every direction trying to reclaim reality. Another whisper.

He looked out at the crowd, and they were on fire. The audience was now a canvas of disembodied, incinerating skulls, black teeth bared, eyeless, laughing at him.

Pervis felt the room spinning and yet his feet were immobile, locked to the stage floor as he stared out into the flaming abyss of floating, laughing charred skulls. He tried to scream, and his throat could only muster a feeble rush of toneless air. A final insult, he thought. He couldn't scream, couldn't run, couldn't control any aspect of this nightmare. His heart...

"*Three!*" came a whisper.

He collapsed to the floor, seeing and feeling nothing.

Only seconds later by his estimation he was staring up at the stage lights and surrounded by concerned strangers telling him to lie still. He was fully clothed except for a rip across the front of his shirt, and the only sounds he could hear was a nervous murmuring from a small group of people a short distance away. Nothing, as far as he could tell, was crawling on him.

"Relax, you're gonna be okay," said one of the good Samaritans standing above him. He sounded British. "Your chest is going to hurt a bit. I had to give you CPR."

Pervis turned his head toward the sound of the voice. The face he saw was familiar, but he couldn't place it.

And the long-haired man gave him a wink.

Chien Sauvage

They met online for the same reason everyone else meets online, for the quick, convenient fulfillment of private fantasies.

Bruce, or "brufitness" as he is known in the masquerade of internet chat rooms, was feeling his hormones boiling over once again, and sought to feed his sugary sexual appetite by trolling through "The Mingler" looking for easy companionship.

He didn't lie about his appearance like most of his cyber-competition. He was actually 30, had closely cropped dark hair and radiant green eyes and a face that many have mistaken for Jean-Claude Van Damme in his prime. His body was lean and muscular, the type of body one would expect of a wide receiver on a professional football team, or of a fitness instructor, which he was. Bruce liked sleek, fast cars but owned a Ford SUV. He liked gangsta rap music and wearing his hat backwards, but would never dream of killing another human being. But mainly he liked women, especially the blonde, blue-eyed, artificially enhanced mainstream babes of his pornographic dreams, those living Barbie dolls who bounced, giggled, got drunk and talked dirty. Like his wife used to do.

In the chat rooms, no one ever looked for the ring on his finger, and that bit of information was never volunteered. No one asks and no one tells, and what happens, happens.

On this night, he took particular interest in a fresh-faced nineteen-year-old named "chiensauvage" who, according to her bio, wanted to "hook up with an older guy" and lived only six miles away from where he and his wife made their home. The picture next to her name aroused him in a delicious way; along with her dirty blonde shoulder-length locks and shimmering blue eyes she wore a smile that whispered invitation and begged for satisfaction…full, pink-painted lips seductively spread to reveal perfect white teeth, a lustful picture of innocence and experience.

"nice name. r u a savage?" he typed.

"mmmmmm...kinda" Smiley face.

In the study, away from the prying eyes of his sleeping wife, Bruce carried on a conversation with the beautiful ingénue on the desktop given to him as a Christmas gift. They talked about their vocations (she was a struggling college student and an aspiring model), their favorite colors (she loved pink), their real names (hers was Didi), and what they liked to do in bed.

"so whatr u doing tonite?"

"ntg" she answered, and then added, "waiting 4 u"

Bruce licked his lips. "u wanna party?"

The Crawlspace

"hell yah the moon is full"

"do u only party on a full moon?"

"no just love the moon it makes me hot lol"

"weird things happen under a full moon" Bruce added a devil emoticon.

"i know"

They arranged to meet at one of Bruce's favorite hot spots, a posh dance club on the east side where good-looking late-night partiers went to be seen and loved.

They chatted for a few minutes more and said goodbye. Bruce quietly put on some decent clothes and brushed his hair. The Nitro club would be perfect. If Didi was underage, she wouldn't be allowed in, and if she wasn't as gorgeous as she led him to believe, she wouldn't show up. Even if Didi was a bust, he could still enjoy a night out on the town with his choice of similar beauties. But he was hoping she was the real McCoy.

He peeked into the bedroom at his wife before he left, and he believed that she was asleep. He could see her in the darkness of their bedroom, the most lavish room of their humble, two-story condo on the western edge of town. If she woke up and called him on his cell, he wouldn't answer, and would later explain that he was with a new client at the gym (it was open 24 hours, a perfect cover). He stared at her for a few seconds, trying to ignore the guilty pangs in his gut. For reasons only he could understand, he didn't consider it cheating. He closed the door gently and headed for the garage.

He thought he heard a rustling as the door shut, but he assumed it was just Sara shifting under the covers.

Didi was neither underage nor deceptive, and she showed up right when she said she would. Amid the semi-darkness and the din of pounding bass and spinning disco lights they found each other, and the attraction was mutual.

She was wearing a head-turning, turquoise blue party dress that revealed what she wanted to reveal. Her hair seemed to shimmer and flow like the girls in the shampoo commercials on TV. "Bruce!" she shouted, beaming and waving to him.

From the moment he recognized her, Bruce put his arm around her shoulder as if claiming her from a pit of well-dressed scavengers, taking care not to spill his bottle of Sam Adams. "Didi! Pleased to meet you!" he said.

"Oh my God, you're gorgeous!" she giggled, and then she kissed him on the lips, a move that was surprising to Bruce, but not unwelcome.

When their lips separated, he noticed she was trembling, and there was nothing resembling a draft in the sweaty, bustling nightclub. "You're not nervous, are you?" he asked.

"No, not at all!" Didi adjusted her necklace, a diamond strand with a studded centerpiece of a triangle inside a circle.

The Crawlspace

"'*Chien Sauvage.*' I love that chat name! French, right?"

"Yeah! It means 'wolf.' Well, 'wild dog' literally, but that's what they call a wolf. I think it's cool."

When he asked her if she'd ever been to France, Bruce took notice of her eyes. They were certainly as blue as her picture had shown, but in person they seemed…they *felt* different. There was a dangerous sparkle, a glint of recklessness and hunger within that seductive shade of Mayan blue, and Bruce could only see it as a kind of sexual urgency…a superficial variation of love at first sight.

That sparkle *was* actually something different, something her victims routinely failed to recognize.

"I wanna dance," Didi said, still trembling, still smiling that smile. She took him by the hand and led him to the dance floor.

Sara was a beautiful woman, trim and strawberry blonde; so beautiful a decent man would never take her for granted. She knew her husband was desirable and how he spent his days watching women bend and grunt and stretch in tight-fitting clothes, so it wasn't unreasonable for her to suspect him of going astray. They talked about it at times, and Bruce always managed to charm his way out of the conversation and the subject was buried along with other hot-button topics like children and vacations. She kept her frustrations and her unhappiness in that same buried place, and the restless nature of those feelings left her unable to sleep most nights, like this night when, after hearing her husband shuffling around the house and the garage door grinding open and closed, she got up out of bed and plopped down in front of the computer in the study.

She was surprised to find it in hibernate mode, still signed on under Bruce's nickname. The instant messenger, which she rarely used except in brief conversations with family, was still activated as well and connected to a chat room called "The Mingler."

For a moment, she had forgotten why she was sitting in front of the computer in the first place. The wave of dread that suddenly crashed on her made the task of checking her mail seem pointless. It wasn't the thought of her husband cheating on her that made her angry (she had prepared herself for that), but the thought of how she would react, what she would do to confront him, what he deserved, what would make her feel better. She hated those thoughts; they frightened her.

She opened up the message archive, and blood rose into her cheeks.

There was only one reason why Bruce was hiking along a trail on Castle Butte at 2:00 in the morning with Didi at his side: he wouldn't get laid any other way tonight. She asked him to drive them here, with the promise of making love under the moonlight.

As they made their way up the trail and trekked further into an area no one should go at night, Bruce was moderating the debate between his two brains.

The Crawlspace

The one below his belt argued that this lovely, stacked blonde was too attractive and too accommodating to let go. At the club, she danced and grinded with a powerful grace, sending a clear message of what she wanted and who she wanted it from. Many of the other men, and most of the other women, couldn't take their eyes off her. She made him feel like royalty. He couldn't let her go now. Besides, this would be a new experience for him, cheaper than a motel and less cramped than the back of the car.

His upper brain was concerned with Didi's strange behavior, her obsession with the full moon in particular. There was something not quite right about her; her jitteriness, the wicked gleam in her eye, her quirky conversation, her not-quite-wholesome smile. He couldn't put a finger on what was making him so uneasy, but as the rocks pinched his feet beneath the soles of his expensive dress shoes, her unusual request was beginning to look more like a bad idea every minute.

The brain on his neck was winning the argument.

"Hey, Didi, why don't we just do it in the car?" he said. "I'll open the sunroof and you'll be able to see the moon."

"C'mon, we're almost there!" She was holding her stiletto heels in her hand, walking the trail barefoot. "It'll be so much better out here," she cooed. "It'll be magic!"

"Don't those rocks hurt your feet?"

She turned and smiled again. "No, nothing hurts. Nothing hurts at all."

"But what if we get stranded up here or something?"

"I know my way down. I've been here a few times." Didi trembled again, inhaling through her teeth with a clean, audible hiss. "God, look at that!" The moon was in mid-sky to the southeast, full, grey and radiant. Spectacular.

Bruce was impressed and nervous all at once. He looked to the horizon at the plains illuminated by the moonlight and took note of the thickness of the desert vegetation that stretched for miles along the base of the mountain. He couldn't see the diamondback rattlers and coyotes rummaging among the brush, but he knew they were there, and a grisly image of them eating him alive began to cross his mind. He'd had enough.

"Look, Didi, this is stupid. Let's turn around."

"Too late," Didi said through hissing gulps of breath, "we're already here!"

She had led him to a sharp turn in the trail curtained by a wall of rock and brush, a shady resting point in the day. She took Bruce by the hand and guided him to the other side of the wall, and Bruce noticed something dripping from her fingernails, as though her nail paint was melting.

"You were so awesome tonight," she sighed. "God, I want you." Didi wrapped her arms around him. Bruce thought he heard her make a sound like a cross between a soft moan and a dog-like snarl, unsure whether it was born from sexual pleasure or deep, gnawing pain.

The Crawlspace

Strange noises echoed from above their heads. Grunting, growling. Hungry sounds that were animal and human. "Do you hear that?" he said.

"Yes! YES!"

Bruce looked at her face and the whole world went cold. It wasn't the same face he saw for the first time at the upscale nightclub hours before. Her eyes were no longer small and blue, but thick and black as night. Her smooth complexion was now rippled with purple, spider-web veins that mimicked the aftermath of a deep bruise, and those veins branched out and multiplied and pulsed under her skin. She still had that sexy, come-hither smile, only now it was teeming with blood-stained saliva dripping from her teeth. Her teeth...*longer?*

Heaving and panting, she pulled him closer. Her bleeding fingernails dug into the back of his neck and a low, guttural moan vibrated from her bleeding lips as she kissed him. Bruce felt the sting, tasted her blood, tasted mortal fear.

He slammed the heel of his hand against her chin and pushed her to the ground, and ran in what he thought was the direction of his car. "Mmmm, yessss!" he heard her scream as if the words were razors in her throat.

As he ran across, then off the trail, he could only think about the inadequacy of his shoes on the rocky terrain, and of the blood on his clothes. Then the horror of Didi's face crashed like a crescendo in his brain, and he ran faster, not entirely sure of where he was go-

Darryl Dawson

ing. He turned to look behind him just to see if she was coming after him.

She was, and so were the others…dozens of them… howling and moaning, bruise-skinned and bleeding, hungry and deceptively fast. They were sliding down the mountainside, picking up his scent.

Bruce was too out-of-breath to scream, so he just kept running. For Bruce there was only the moonlight and the howling and the sour taste of blood and the sounds of his footsteps on the desert floor. He held on to all of them for as long as he could.

Sara wasn't sure what to do now. She had driven to the Nitro club, saw Bruce leaving with the blonde girl, followed her husband's car all the way out to Castle Butte and had just finished crying. She thought about just going home and waiting for him there, but the thought of him with that young tramp made her more agitated. She decided she would not allow him the chance to lie his way out of this one. She had to find him; she wasn't sure what she would do or say when she found him, but it had to be done.

She stepped out of the car and looked over the hillside to the plains below. Only a lunatic would be out here in the middle of the night, she angrily mused. She grabbed a flashlight out of the trunk of her car and started walking.

She heard strange noises in the distance, and assumed they were coyotes.

Yellow

Yellow...Red.

I don't envy the life of a traffic light. Everything is so regimented, so perfectly timed, enslaved by a computer program buried in a steel box. It's not what I wanted, but what choice do I have now?

This shall be my residence until he returns. He won't expect me here. It's perfect.

Green.

All you heading east and west, get going! Go on to your jobs, your shopping, the schools of your children. Get to the places you need to be while you can because there might come a time when someone will carelessly end your life, and you will find yourself going no place, being no one. This is where I'm at now, and it's no fun at all.

Darryl Dawson

This intersection, this busy, dirty crucifix of asphalt, is now my responsibility. I inhabit the traffic light on the northwest corner, and what used to be my eyes now survey the flow of mindless cars rumbling along the street.

Yellow...Red.

I am at the mercy of the computer for now. When it tells me to give the appropriate signal, the electrical impulses are fired through the wires of my new body, igniting the light bulbs at the top of my head. But there is a way to override that program and control the signals myself, and I'm figuring out how to do so. When the time comes I'll be able to switch a red to a green a few seconds early, or shorten the transition from yellow to red, altering the course of traffic, watching the cars smash.

Green.

I've been practicing. So far any accidents that have happened in my intersection haven't been caused by me. No, more likely by the thoughtless ones, the drivers who pick up that cup of coffee or answer their cell phone at the worst possible time, or who just have their minds elsewhere. Much like the one who killed me.

The Crawlspace

I can still see the makeshift cross on the northeast corner erected by the sidewalk in my honor, so I know it hasn't been long since my death, but I can't say how long it's been because my sense of time has been severely altered. My memory of the accident itself is still vivid and I can still see the face of the driver. That stupid kid.

Red. Whoa!...Yellow...Red. God, how it angers me.

I was a pedestrian trying to cross the street to get to the bus stop, trying to get to work on time. I vaguely remember running...seeing the bus parked at the stop with no passengers boarding or leaving. It was about to take off, I was sure of it. I had to catch it. Then I heard the squealing of brakes and felt an impact that turned me sideways and shattered both my legs at the knees. That moment...staring into the windshield...it feels like a sunspot.

His face was so young, a teenager's perhaps. His sunglasses flew up off his nose and I could see his eyes, sharp blue and wide with terror. His dark brown, shaggy hair almost seemed to stand on end and his mouth formed a perfect circle. It felt like I was staring at him for several seconds, but time was like water trying to seep through a clogged drain. Then I couldn't see him anymore. Glass penetrated my skin and my head felt soft. Then there was nothing.

Darryl Dawson

Green.

The body I used to occupy is buried somewhere in this county. It used to walk the earth like you, preoccupied with the joys, problems, wonders and heartache that come with life. Now I feel incomplete and coiled with anger. I'm not sure if heaven or hell awaits me; really, I'm not sure if I'm in heaven or hell already. But this afterlife that I must now accept must be part of some larger plan. Perhaps leaving my spirit here at the intersection where it was separated from my body will help me find relief from this sense of unresolved matters. I guess this is what happens when you die angry.

This street, and the horizons on either side, are the extent of the range of my vision, but that is all I need to see. I can see the cars passing under me, and in each car I can see the driver. Singing along to the radio, carrying on conversations with passengers, keeping their children quiet...I see them all. And I recognize one.

He's a young man with dark brown hair and a brand new pair of sunglasses. He takes this road eastbound to somewhere every day. That stupid kid. I can't forget his face. And one day...

Yellow.

Red.

Closing Time At Teddie's

Tonight was Mel DeVoto's birthday...his thirtieth...and riding through the dark and dangerous streets of Phoenix's Southside in an unwashed Cutlass, he could feel the minor alcohol buzz wearing off from the informal party thrown on his behalf just minutes ago. He never was much of a drinker; he always limited himself to one or two beers, even on special nights like tonight, not because he disliked alcohol, but because he was afraid of being out of control.

The radio was playing a favorite R & B song from his youth when he pulled into the parking lot of Teddie's Topless Nightclub, a place he would find time to visit once or twice a month whenever he had the spare change and the pangs of loneliness. Mel preferred this place to the "Gentlemen's Clubs" of Downtown and Scottsdale because it was dirtier, cheaper and thoroughly lacking in extravagance. Teddie's was a taut, square building with milk-white windowless walls, not too distinguishable from the pawn shops and *panderías* nearby, and tonight it featured a fresh attack of graffiti. Over the front was hung a barely-working neon box with the name "Teddie's" painted in script over a poorly-drawn imitation of a scantily clad Vargas Girl, all framed with big, pink light bulbs flashing in alternating motion. Social critics would kindly call it "tacky," but for Mel, it was perfect. This was, after all, a strip club; a place where women rub their naked bodies on aroused men for dollar bills. He felt there should be no elegance in such a place, and Teddie's was the only club in the city that understood that. This was 1989, a time when men didn't go to strip clubs to impress people. In fact many would find it odd or even a bit pitiful that a good-looking, college-educated Black man in the prime of his life would spend the waning hours of his birthday in a flesh den on the bad side of town. Mel tried not to think so.

He cut the radio off in mid-chorus as he pulled into the space closest to the front door. His was the one car that saved the parking lot from being completely empty, not counting a small group of cars huddled in the rear of the building that most likely belonged to the employees. Hip-hop rumbled from behind the wooden doors as he walked in, his I.D. already in his hand for the bouncer to verify.

Mel quickly realized he was the only paying customer in the entire place, and he nearly turned tail and walked back out, but changed his mind, allowing himself just one interactive experience and maybe a drink. The LED on his watch showed "10:55." Usually there was a least a handful of patrons at this late hour, even on a Thursday night.

He stood to the side of the bar behind the random settings of tables and chairs, staring out at the empty stage with its lonely brass pole rooted like a dead tree in a flat hill covered in wood paneling. The walls were plum-colored and decorated with torch-like lamps with dull shades and paintings of nude black women posing with white tigers. A layer of black and white tiles turned the floor into a massive, shiny chess board. It looked like the living room of a pimp in a 70's blaxploitation movie. The D.J. booth was missing its master of ceremonies, though the sexy, bass-heavy beats continued to pump through the speakers in his absence. Mel gently nodded his head to the rhythm, silently wondering why the room was so dead. The sign on the door said they were open until two a.m.

An attractive, Rubenesque woman in her forties wearing a t-shirt and jeans approached him. "Can I get you something?" she asked.

"Just a Coke," he replied, pulling off his jacket.

The waitress smirked and with a hint of well-intentioned sarcasm remarked, "You got here just in time, sweetie." She walked back to the bar to get his Coke.

Yeah, thought Mel, *just before closing up early. Nice timing.* He took a seat right in front of the stage and waited for the first performer.

The waitress came back with a glass loaded with more ice than cola and set it down on the stage in front of him. "Four dollars," she said, glancing at her watch.

Mel felt a little embarrassed bringing it up over a four-dollar soft drink, but that's what this special day was for. "It's my birthday today."

The smirk returned to her face. "Yeah, that's what they all say. How many of those have you had this month?"

"No, really, I turned thirty." He reached into his back pocket to pull out his I.D. again.

"Just yanking your chain, honey. It's on the house." She checked her watch again. "But you're not getting any free lap dances, alright?"

"Yeah, yeah, that's cool." He reached instead into his front pocket and pulled out a dollar for her tip. "When are the dancers coming on?"

"She'll be on in a little bit. There's just one dancer tonight, but she's really good. You'll like her."

"What happened? Did everybody go home?"

The waitress turned her eyes toward one of the velvet erotic paintings on the wall. "Well, yeah. I sent most of my girls home. I didn't want to risk..." She stopped herself. "I mean, it's kinda dead right now. No need to have them here, really."

"Funny you mention that. Why am I the only guy here at eleven o'clock?"

The waitress checked her watch again, even after he had told her the time. The look of anxiety on her face sparked a concerned curiosity in Mel.

"It's just a slow night, that's all."

Mel pressed her. "C'mon, what happened? Did you guys get in trouble or something?"

"No, it's nothing like that, it's..."

"It's what?"

The Crawlspace

The woman sighed and put her hand to her forehead as though she was about to reveal some dark, incriminating secret, then looked at him with grave seriousness. "Tonight's the night she comes back," she said.

"What do you mean? Who's coming back?"

The waitress pulled up a chair and sat next to him. "How old did you say you were?"

"Thirty."

"You might be old enough to remember. Ever hear the story of what happened here fifteen years ago?"

He shook his head. "I wasn't living here back then."

"Oh. Well, one of our dancers got murdered here. A real sweet girl, a college girl...and man, could she dance. Gorgeous body, and not shy in the least. She had regular customers lined up to see her. And off the floor, one of the nicest people you'd ever want to meet. She was...magnetic, you know? Seemed like everybody had a crush on her, including my husband. Her name was Marilyn. I remember once she told me, 'My boyfriend has no idea I do this for a living. He thinks I'm pulling a night shift at the Denny's down the street!' She laughed about it." She swallowed and continued: "Do you get jealous?"

"Jealous? I don't know. I don't think so."

"If you found out your girlfriend was working in this place, what would you do? C'mon, be honest."

He shrugged his shoulders. Mel never had girlfriends; he had company. For him, relationships required a level of detachment suitable for a mortician. "I guess I'd dump her."

"Right, there you go," she said. "That's what most guys would do. Well, Marilyn's boyfriend came in one night with a bag from one of those fancy department stores. Nobody bothered to check what was in it."

The waitress's voice began to waver with a small measure of regret. "He asked where her dressing room was, and somebody showed him. A minute later we heard two gunshots. Didn't know if they came from outside or inside. The guy was just running out when we started to smell gasoline, then smoke. Everybody cleared out. I ran in to try to get her out of there, but…" She stopped, fighting the urge to cry, unable to finish that part of the story. "They caught the boyfriend and arrested him, and now he's rotting in Lewis Prison. The bastard should've fried." She looked straight into his eyes. "You know what they found out at the trial? The bullets didn't kill her. He shot her twice in the back, but she was still alive when he set her on fire."

She turned her eyes back to the floor and shook her head, pondering the gravity of what she was about to say. "She never left. My husband and I have tried everything. New paint job, new name, new furniture. But I swear to God, she's still here. Every now and again *her* song would start playing on the P.A. system. That's when we all know she's here."

Just then, the music stopped. "What song?" Mel asked, startled by the sudden crash of silence.

"Some old soul song. Ever hear of a song called 'Natural High'? I forget who sings it."

The Crawlspace

Bloodstone, he warmly remembered to himself.

"She loved that song, loved dancing to it. Man, she put everything she had into that performance, like she was making love to the song, y'know what I mean? I used to love that song, too. Now it makes me sick. I can't even listen to it anymore. It just kills me. There's no trace of that record anywhere in this building, but every year on this day *it plays by itself!* It feels kind of slow and garbled like the record's warped, but it's Marilyn's song. 'Natural High.'" She stared off at the empty stage, her voice growing colder with the memory. "Five years ago, it came on real loud while a girl was on this stage. She started shaking like she was having a fit. Then her back just snapped in half."

A new song suddenly popped on, shattering the tension. The lights on the stage faded up to reveal a short, thin brunette wearing a powder blue lingerie ensemble, ready to begin her provocative routine. Mel was still staring with disbelief at the woman who served him his ice-heavy beverage.

"And I know she's coming back again, tonight," she said, barely audible over the musical din refilling the room. She checked her watch yet again. "We gotta close at midnight. No later."

Mel watched her wipe tears from her face as she walked back to the bar, her bizarre recollection flashing in his mind like the old, neon sign outside. He was confused and more than a little disturbed, but as he devoted more of his attention to the slinky nymph thrusting and bouncing just for him, the creepy feeling faded out, giving way to an assumption that maybe she was just talking shit. It didn't stop him from taking a quick glance at his watch between gyrations.

It was eleven-thirty-one.

The dancer, who introduced herself as Leticia, performed her exclusive act for another ten minutes and Mel tipped her well. She was as the waitress advertised; coordinated, flexible and irresistible, though her face was just flawed enough to keep her from plying her trade at the more popular strip clubs. She had already gathered her tips and clothes and stowed them away backstage, and was now seated next to Mel, hoping to make the most of a dull and barely profitable evening.

Mel played the birthday card with the almost-naked vixen. "Aw, happy birthday!" she cooed, hugging him like a boyfriend. "I wish I had a gift for you, but I don't!"

"You can give me a lap dance," Mel suggested.

Leticia giggled. "Only if you got 25 bucks!"

Mel feigned disappointment, making her laugh out loud. He knew it was a stretch. "Alright," he said, pulling a twenty and a five from his pocket, saving another twenty for her tip. They made their way back to the area known as the Chardonnay room, between the dressing rooms and the bar. The waitress was already standing in the doorway with her arms crossed.

"This area's closed," she stated, "and you got five minutes."

She and Leticia argued over policies, procedures and superstitions, but the forty-something lady's word was final, and she was locking the door. She did so and cued up a song in the DJ booth, sounding one last five-minute warning.

Mel took a seat in the middle of the room, amused and impressed with how serious the waitress was taking her story. The music began, and Leticia was calm enough to put on her smile and disrobe down to her blue thong and high heels. She would perform her services with slinky precision, purring in his ear and humping his crotch to the rhythm. Mel became absorbed in the heat of her fabricated seduction.

She was seated in his lap when his eyes turned to the floor. A small puff of grey smoke was crawling along the ground like a drop of mercury. The stereo speakers crackled with intermittent static. The ball of smoke settled under Leticia's feet. The music stopped with a loud pop.

"That wasn't no five minutes!" she yelled to no response. Then a new song began--a nauseating, incongruous blend of crying violins and demonic four-part harmonies in the slow cadence of a warped vinyl record. It was "Natural High" as heard in a nightmare.

Mel's lust was overlapped by nervous tension. Leticia just sat in his lap, confused and…shuddering. Choking sounds came from the back of her throat as her body jerked. Her head snapped up and down with inhuman force, leaving jaw-shaped bruises on her bare chest. Bones snapped in her neck and blood dripped from her nose. She was dead.

And then her head swayed back and forth. And the evil swirl of music played.

Darryl Dawson

Mel screamed and tried to push her off of him, but her hands reached back and grabbed his shirt. The chair fell backwards and she fell on top of him. He could hear the waitress screaming behind him, saying something that sounded like, "Marilyn!" The calliope of death was louder, overwhelming, droning in the ears of everyone inside. Mel looked at the tilted head of the corpse holding on to him.

Behind the smoldering scars was a face of pure rage.

He punched her arms and chest until her grip released and her lifeless body fell off to the side. Covered in her smoky scent, he bolted for the door. He pushed it, pulled it, slammed his shoulder against it. It wouldn't move.

"The door!" he screamed. "Somebody unlock the door!" He looked for the waitress, and saw her lying on the floor, motionless.

He also saw Leticia standing up. Her nude body was horribly singed, her head was tilted at a gruesome angle and her face spoke of violent revenge. Mel knew she had to be dead, and what he was seeing couldn't be possible. But she was trying to walk, extending a single outstretched arm to him. He froze.

He was grabbed from behind by a large man wearing a black t-shirt. The bouncer had used his key to open the door, and they both ran out, leaving the monstrous tune jangling in the distance behind them.

The Crawlspace

Mel DeVoto lay under the covers of his bed with his eyes open, his foggy head covered to the ears with a well-worn comforter. The memory made him too frightened to sleep, and after hours of wringing his body between the sheets in a futile attempt to find slumber, he had simply given up. Not even watching some disposable late-night TV could filter the hellish thoughts from his mind. The darkness mocked him, pulled him into the grip of that inescapable night terror that made him feel as though closing his eyelids would kill him. The dawn would not come soon enough nor offer any guarantee of relief. Between short gulps of breath, he silently cursed the ugly strip club, Marilyn, and the birthday years ago he would never forget.

And today was his birthday. His fiftieth.

Connecting Flight

CANCELLED. CANCELLED. CANCELLED.

Jacob Tremmer had seen the word again and again in dull red vertical stacks on all the video screens at Kansas City International Airport, and it depressed him. It meant more time waiting in lines and lounges until someone somewhere said they could get on a plane and go back home. The Christmas holiday was almost over and for the Tremmer family, and many of the jilted travelers standing beside them in line for a hotel voucher, snow was no longer beautiful or romantic.

Boredom is the mortal enemy of children, and Jacob was eight years old and very, very bored. Not quite exasperated like his stepmother, not at all scared like his three-year-old sister, and by no means simmering with red frustration like his father--just bored. Stuck on the ground.

Jacob, a studious but handsome child with dark almond skin, bided the time by sitting cross-legged on the floor reading his favorite book, "Space Heroes," immersing himself in the stories of the Apollo missions and the first Space Shuttles and the brave men and women who led the way into the dark, starry territories beyond earth, some of whom didn't make it back. These were the most compelling dramas of his young life, inspiring to the last.

His father would sometimes say to him, "You can't be an astronaut. You're not smart enough." His step mom was more politely dismissive, finding it cute that he was so interested in "flying around in the dark," as she put it.

As Jacob read his book, the bright, cavernous terminal echoed with a chorus of low chatter that was occasionally overridden by polite, conciliatory announcements on the public address system. The tangled lines of conversation were mostly negotiations—with hotels, with rental car companies, with the airline—but beneath it all were the sounds of commiserating travelers reaching the undisputed consensus that airports are hell. Jacob stopped and listened. The voices blended all together in a busy stew of pleasant concessions and intense demands and all in-between. Jacob found it noisy and disconcerting and he wanted to block it all out. He knew what it would lead to but he didn't care. He set his book down and stood up, then closed his eyes and went searching for the warm, silent place.

He lifted ever-so-slightly. The soles of his basketball shoes began to separate from the floor until he was an inch above it. He couldn't hear the airport anymore. The back of his neck tingled as if a powerful energy was taking it in its jaws like a lioness grabbing a cub. He felt calm and peaceful, but he wanted to stop. He opened his eyes and took a quick breath, and gravity took him by the shoes and yanked him back to earth. Everything was noisy and boring again. The line moved, and he and his family moved closer to the ticket counter.

Jacob was only a month old when he realized he could psychokinetically levitate.

He was alone with his birth mother in the old house when he felt the strange sensation for the first time, just before falling asleep. All he remembered was being startled after bouncing off the mattress of his crib, but little else.

He was certain he was in the presence of his mother when it happened again, because it was her screaming that sent him crashing back down in a heap onto the white shag carpet. It didn't hurt much, but the jolt made him howl in infant terror. It terrorized him more that his mother made no effort to console him; she just stood there with her arms in the air and a wild expression on her face, gasping for breath and hollering in some strange language about "mercy" and "Satan." She then grabbed him and ran into the bathroom and shoved his face into a toilet.

The feeling of being stuffed with water, of darkness, of cold porcelain, of shame, lasted only for a moment before someone pulled him out, and he lay on the bathmat coughing and crying. There was more yelling, more ugly noises without translation, and then he saw his father's face slackened in helpless worry as he gathered him in his giant hands.

He never saw his mother again after that. He didn't understand, but somehow he felt like whatever happened was his fault. Out of fear, he made sure he never did it again. Not until he found out what an astronaut was.

He wasn't born yet when Challenger exploded, and was too young to grasp the second tragedy of Columbia. He arrived upon his love for space travel with the fascination and *naïveté* of all childhood romanticism. His eyes locked on the images beamed back from space of astronauts in their marshmallow suits floating and tinkering outside the space station, the first ones to walk after Columbia. In school he learned about gravity and the planets and our first trip to the moon and fully understood what he was and what he was meant to be...a space traveler. He was born floating; it was in his nature. It was his destiny to explore the sky and the stars, to do cartwheels in midair, to use meteorites as stepping stones. The thought brought back the tingle to the nape of his neck, and the fear was gone. He was inside the house when he blocked everything out and let go, guided upward by the soft undulation until his body rested against the ceiling. Here, he was in space, locked inside a cool, black tranquility that no-one could share. Roger, Houston. One small step...

He nearly crashed to the floor as he felt a sudden yank on his belt buckle. His father was there to grab him and settle him back down onto the itchy carpet.

"Now you listen to me," he said, the rage from his eyes fixing Jacob taut against the floor. "Don't *ever* do that again! Not around me, not around anybody! Outside, inside, I don't give a damn! You could end up hurting yourself, you could freak somebody out. That

The Crawlspace

ain't natural, and you know that! *Never* do that again! You hear me?"

Jacob nodded, silently hating his gift, hating his need to fly, and knew that his father would go away too if he ever tried it again.

But he did just now, in the crowded airport terminal, behind his father's back. And nothing happened this time.

"We're taking the first flight out of this goddamn mess," his father muttered, the muscles in his temples keeping time. He was tall, fit Black man with little humor and less patience.

Jacob's stepmother, a curvy redhead in her early thirties, carried his red-headed little sister (now sleeping after a lengthy and dramatic crying session) in her arms like a paper sack of groceries. "The next flight out probably isn't going to happen 'til tomorrow morning," she reasoned. "Maybe tomorrow afternoon. Look out the window."

His dad didn't look, but Jacob did. Outside the snow was measured in feet, still coming down fast in the amber-illuminated darkness, gathering on the still, silent jets parked on the white tarmac while trucks cleared paths as best they could. Jacob stared.

Outside was grandma and her warm house and her warm smile and her warm, sweet apricot pie. Grandma, who always gave him space-related toys for Christmas and let him play with them on her shiny wood floor, and had no idea that all those toys would disappear as soon as he got home to L.A., replaced by toy trucks or big, clumsy water guns. Grandma, who was in Jefferson City, only a two-hour drive from the airport.

I wonder how long it would take for me to fly, Jacob thought. *Here to Jefferson City. Floating. How long? And how cold is it out there really?*

"Put that book away!" he heard his father say with unmistakable sternness. He closed it and zipped it up in the front compartment of his kid-sized travel bag.

"Can I go to the bathroom?"

"No," his dad shot back. "We have to wait here. I don't want you wandering off."

His step mom interjected. "C'mon, Leeman, the bathroom's right there. It's no big deal!"

"We're all staying here!" Dad said. "Our turn's coming up."

"Oh, for Pete's sake, Leeman, the kid's gotta pee!" She stooped down to talk to Jacob, little sis' still draped across her chest. "You see that bathroom over there? You use that, then come straight back, okay? Don't talk to nobody, and if anybody tries to grab you, scream real loud and Daddy and I will come get you, understand?"

"He ain't goin' to no bathroom, Rae!"

"Let him go!" She seemed to punch his father with those words, then turned back to Jacob. "You do as I say, understand me?"

"Yes, ma'am." Jacob stood his bag up on its wheel's end and took another quick glance at the snow outside the window. His jacket was still tied around his waist.

How cold? He ran toward the restroom, not more than fifty feet away.

How cold? How far?

He used the urinal, washed his hands and stepped out to hear a commotion rumbling in the terminal. Dad and Step mom were causing a scene that brought the crowd to a voyeuristic standstill; screaming, gesticulating, swearing, threatening--another one of their "discussions." Security was called in to calm things down. Little sister was screaming again.

He ran.

Sneaking below the preoccupied radars of the airport's imprisoned populace, Jacob rushed to the other side of Terminal A's semi-circle and snuck outside to the nearly-empty drop-off area. No one talked to him or grabbed him.

He came to a chain link fence that separated him from the tarmac. On the other side the planes stood still, their logos partially covered with snow. It was only 7:30, but it felt like midnight. Silent, dark, a little scary. And more than a little cold.

He pulled the wool beanie and gloves from the inside pockets of his jacket and put them on. The jacket was on next, zipped. He looked up at the charcoal grey darkness and felt the snow flutter down onto his face and became less afraid of both of them. He thought of Grandma again and worked himself into a mild, undulating calm, then...

"Jacob Tremmer, please pick up the white courtesy phone. Jacob Tremmer, please pick up the white courtesy phone."

He thought about them, Dad and Stepmom, for a moment, and how worried they must be. Maybe it's best to go back inside. Dad's probably mad, so mad he'd take his Christmas toys away and not replace them with anything, maybe even give him the belt. And then he looked up into the cloudy night again.

Just a few minutes ago, he thought, *they were only thinking of themselves.*

"Jacob Tremmer, please pick up the white courtesy phone..."

He blocked out the robotic P.A. voice, the gentle night sounds of a snowbound airport, everything. His head became a silent, empty tomb. The back of his neck tingled...stronger...

Liftoff.

In the silence, in the darkness, in the cover of heavy snow, he floated into the air unnoticed. It was time to find Grandma.

Jacob drifted with the influence of the wind, unburdened and sheltered in the blissful sanctuary of all the best recollections of Christmas. The warm, spicy smells of the kitchen, the happy songs on the stereo, and the soothing voice of his grandmother as she read to him stories of Santa, Jesus Christ and little kids in space before tucking him into bed. His whole body

The Crawlspace

was aglow in goodness, and time seemed to stretch into immeasurable segments.

And then he wondered where he was, how close he was to Jefferson City. He opened his eyes.

The dark clouds were now below him, obscuring his view of the ground. He had no idea where he was. The air suddenly felt colder; little chunks of ice were stinging his face. The tingling in the back of his neck stopped, and he began to fall.

Twisting in the air, that roller-coaster feeling in his stomach, he dropped below the surface of the clouds and saw only darkness. His jaw slacked open. His eyes ached from the onslaught of icy air. Falling, fast. No Dad. No Stepmom. No Grandma. Only a rising, spreading darkness.

He closed his eyes and balled his hands into fists and tried to shut it all out. The loopy, sick feeling in his stomach was making it hard, but he tried. He grit his teeth. "Up On The Housetop." Grandma. Apricot pie. Merry Christmas, Grandma. Click-click-click.

The tingling started to come back to his neck, but he wasn't slowing down. Warm, warm. Read to me, Grandma. Warm, warm.

His eyes were shut and his heart was racing. The back of his neck felt like it was rubbed with raw peppermint. He unclenched his fists and gave in.

He didn't know how close he came to the ground before he started to slow down and rise again.

Warm, warm. And even the cold air felt warm.

Jacob was flying again, calmer, more secure, and determined to find Grandma.

He surrounded himself with good thoughts again--the fun and beauty of Christmas and the peaceful sanctity of Jefferson City. He thought of living with Grandma forever, leaving everything in Los Angeles behind. *She needs me more than Dad does,* he thought, *it's only fair. It's a better place. I'll learn all about space and be an astronaut when I grow up. I'll make her proud of me.*

And he floated without direction or care, buoyant in his memories and dreams, for hours that felt like minutes.

The air suddenly felt strange to Jacob; a different cold, a compressing cold. He wondered how close he was again, but he didn't want to fall. Still, he had to know. There was no course plotted, no plan. It was fun but really dangerous. He braced himself and opened his eyes...

...and his mouth fell open in amazement. The neck-tingling stopped.

But he didn't fall. He couldn't.

Above him were stars, a vast spectacle on a canvas of inky black. The stars he would sometimes see on summer nights, tiny glimmers of white gold blinking, fading, sometimes rushing over the bowl of blackness at the speed of a wish. The stars he read about in books, the stars he dreamed about. Only now they were closer, within reach, real.

The Crawlspace

He wanted to laugh, but he couldn't breathe, so Jacob just smiled, reaching his hand out as far as he could to touch the beautiful, twinkling stars. All the stars. And as he became one of them, he thought of Christmas, and Grandma, and warm apricot pie.

About the Author

DARRYL DAWSON is a TV news satellite coordinator and former disc jockey. He was born in Los Angeles in the mid-1960's, raised by teachers in Harbor City, California, and currently resides in Phoenix, Arizona. This is his first book.

LaVergne, TN USA
14 June 2010
186008LV00001B/4/P